"Would you marry me?" Adam asked softly

Lenore was spellbound. The words, *Yes, I would marry you*, formed in her mind, but instead she said defensively, "I've only just met you."

"What I meant was would any woman in her right mind want to marry a half-blind man?"

She was unexpectedly swamped by disappointment because his question had not been a proposal.

"On the other hand," he went on, "I wouldn't mind having a woman to share my bed and match passion with passion." He paused dramatically. "A woman like you."

"You're crazy!" Lenore stuttered as her body played traitor to her will.

"Ever since I found you outside in the snow this afternoon, I've tried to protect you against me," he whispered, "but I can't any more. I want you, and I'm going to have you," he promised as his mouth swooped to hers.

Books by Flora Kidd

HARLEQUIN PRESENTS

309—PASSIONATE ENCOUNTER
327—TOGETHER AGAIN
333—TANGLED SHADOWS
344—STAY THROUGH THE NIGHT
370—THE ARRANGED MARRIAGE
379—THE SILKEN BOND
400—WIFE BY CONTRACT
434—BEYOND CONTROL
447—PERSONAL AFFAIR
464—PASSIONATE STRANGER
485—BRIDE FOR A CAPTAIN
495—MEETING AT MIDNIGHT
520—MAKEBELIEVE MARRIAGE
554—BETWEEN PRIDE AND PASSION
577—TEMPTED TO LOVE
592—DARK SEDUCTION
643—TROPICAL TEMPEST
657—DANGEROUS ENCOUNTER
682—PASSIONATE PURSUIT
729—DESPERATE DESIRE

HARLEQUIN ROMANCES

1865—STRANGER IN THE GLEN
1907—ENCHANTMENT IN BLUE
1977—THE DANCE OF COURTSHIP
1999—THE SUMMER WIFE
2056—THE BLACK KNIGHT
2146—TO PLAY WITH FIRE
2228—THE BARGAIN BRIDE

These books may be available at your local bookseller.

For a list of all titles currently available,
send your name and address to:

Harlequin Reader Service
P.O. Box 52040, Phoenix, AZ 85072-2040
Canadian address: P.O. Box 2800, Postal Station A,
5170 Yonge St., Willowdale, Ont. M2N 5T5

FLORA KIDD

desperate desire

Harlequin Books

TORONTO • NEW YORK • LONDON
AMSTERDAM • PARIS • SYDNEY • HAMBURG
STOCKHOLM • ATHENS • TOKYO • MILAN

Harlequin Presents first edition October 1984
ISBN 0-373-10729-3

Original hardcover edition published in 1984
by Mills & Boon Limited

CHAPTER ONE

Coming out of Northport's small supermarket, her arms full of brown paper grocery bags, Lenore Parini didn't see the man who was approaching the entrance to the store, and she walked right into him.

Knocked off balance, clutching the loaded heavy bags tightly to her chest, afraid she might drop the one containing the eggs, she went staggering back against the door that had closed behind her, bounced off it and fell forward against the man.

He swore viciously and descriptively, leaving her in no doubt about his opinion of her, while his hands grasped her arms bruisingly. Managing somehow to keep his balance, he held her upright until she was once more on an even keel.

Breathless and indignant, she glared up at him. Below fronds of untidy, untrimmed longish ash-blond hair falling across his broad forehead dark frameless glasses glinted down at her instead of eyes. His well-shaped lips curved back from his white teeth in a snarl.

'Why the hell don't you look where you're going?' he grated.

'Why don't you?' Lenore retorted acidly, and turning away from him she marched along the narrow sidewalk towards the junction of Bay Street and Main Street, her long slim legs in their tight-fitting jeans and high brown leather boots seeming to express her irritation with every stride they made.

'Arrogant, chauvinistic pig!' she muttered to herself. 'Who does he think he is? Built like a tank too. I'm probably bruised all over after walking into him!'

Still muttering she turned right up the hill of Main Street, slowing down her pace as she realised the gradient was much more steep than she had anticipated and the bags she was carrying were not only heavy but awkward to hold.

Pale spring sunlight gleamed on the white clapboard of old houses and tall elms striped the roadway with black shadows. Halfway up the street Lenore reached the Northport Inn, an elegant late eighteenth-century building, gable-ended with black shutters edging its long windows, set back from the roadway with a small courtyard in front of it which now served as a car park for guests.

Following a flagged pathway along the side of the house, she went round to the back door. Since her arms were full she couldn't open the door, nor could she ring the bell, so she kicked at it with one foot. It was opened at last by a black-haired, brown-eyed woman of about thirty years of age, Blythe Parini, her elder sister and the owner-manager of the Northport Inn.

'I told you to take the car,' said Blythe, taking some of the bags of groceries and turning away into the wide well lit, well equipped kitchen which was her pride and joy and which she had had remodelled soon after taking over the inn the previous spring. 'I knew there'd be too much for you to carry easily.'

'I got here with them, didn't I?' replied Lenore, setting down the bags she was still carrying beside the others on one of the long wooden counters. She began to unpack one of the bags, taking out the long packages of eggs and opening each one of them and checking for breakages. 'If one of these eggs has so much as a hairline crack, I'll sue him!' she muttered.

'Him?' queried Blythe, raising her eyebrows as she gave her sister an amused but affectionate glance. 'Who's him?'

'The guy I walked into as I was leaving the store. God, was he rude! Tall, a lot of blondish straight hair, hardbitten—know him?'

'Adam Jonson,' said Blythe promptly, also unpacking groceries. From under her lashes she slated a curious glance at her sister. Lenore's thin cheeks, so pale when she had arrived at the inn two days ago, were flushed pink and her big, dark-lashed amber eyes were glittering. Blythe's generously full lips curved in a knowing grin. It seemed there was life left in Lenore yet, in spite of the debilitating illness she had suffered lately.

'So he's notorious,' remarked Lenore dryly.

'For his abrupt manners? Yes.'

'For his *lack* of manners, I'd say. And his abuse of the English language. To say nothing of his opinion of women. Where does he live?'

'In the Jonson house at Pickering Point,' replied Blythe, putting the last of the groceries away and closing the door of the big walk-in fridge.

'Oh.' Lenore looked up. 'One of those Jonsons. I didn't know there were any of them left. Last time I was on holiday here with Mum and Dad,

Martin Jonson died and the house was boarded up. Rumour had it that there weren't any heirs.'

'Rumour was wrong,' said Blythe, filling a cooking pan with water at the sink. 'Adam Jonson is, apparently, the grandson of Martin's younger brother, who left Northport years ago to seek his fortune somewhere. Adam inherited the property when Martin died. He just didn't come to see it or live in it, and Albert Smith looked after it for him.' She put the pan on one of the rings of the electric cooking range. 'Like some coffee and a doughnut before we start preparing dinner for to-night's guests?' she asked.

'Sounds great,' said Lenore, slipping off her quilted down-filled parka and hanging it up behind the kitchen door. She pushed her silky dark brown hair back from her face and sat down at the round maple table that was set before a window.

'He's half blind,' announced Blythe suddenly as she took coffee mugs from a cupboard. 'He was in some sort of accident that left him blind and lame, and he came here to recuperate. Now he can walk pretty well, but he still doesn't see too well. That's probably why he didn't see you coming out of the store and avoid you.'

'Oh, no!' Lenore groaned. 'Oh, what have I done?'

'What's the matter?'

'When we collided he snarled at me and asked me why the hell I didn't look where I was going, so I retaliated with "Why don't you?" Now I feel awful. I wouldn't have snarled back if I'd known he's partially blind.'

'Not like you to snarl, either,' commented Blythe.

'Well, he swore at me and made me mad,' said Lenore defensively. 'He was so arrogant!'

'Mmm, I know what you mean,' murmured Blythe, spooning instant coffee into the two pottery mugs. 'Adam is a tough customer. He's had to be, to live alone out on that point in that old house right through the winter we've just had.'

'Alone? You mean there's been no one else living with him? No one to ... to, well, help him? I guess he needed help when he first came,' said Lenore, her vivid imagination enabling her to empathise with the man she didn't know and with whom her one contact had been brief and rather violent. 'Not to be able to see, not to be able to walk properly when you're young and vital must be one of the worst punishments,' she whispered. 'Oh, how I wish I hadn't said what I did to him!'

'You're the same as ever,' said Blythe. 'Soft-hearted and far too sensitive. There was someone living with Adam at first—a woman,' she added.

'His wife?'

'No. At least, she didn't wear a wedding ring. She used to do the shopping for him, but she didn't talk to anyone much, so we all drew our own conclusions as to what her relationship to him was,' said Blythe dryly. 'But she left just before Christmas. Couldn't stand living in that godforsaken place, I guess.'

'Or couldn't stand living with him,' said Lenore with a sigh. 'But I still wish I hadn't said what I did to him now that I know he can't see too well. Shouldn't he have had a white stick or something?'

'Would you have seen it if he had?' queried Blythe mockingly.

'No, I suppose I wouldn't. I could hardly see over the tops of the bags. Oh, he was right—I wasn't looking where I was going.' Lenore pushed away from the table and went over to the door to take down her jacket and pull it on. 'I'll go right now to find him and apologise,' she said impulsively, zipping up the jacket.

'Lenore, leave it be,' said Blythe, speaking more sharply than she did as a rule. 'Adam Jonson is some proud man, and you'll only make matters worse by rushing up to him in the street and explaining and apologising. You weren't to know that his eyesight is less than perfect, and your retort was perfectly justified. He had no right to be so rude to you.'

Lenore hovered by the back door, hesitating, her fingers curling round the doorknob.

'Besides, he's probably on his way back to Pickering Point by now,' Blythe went on. 'Come and sit down and have this coffee, then you can get to work on preparing the fruit for the dessert I want to make this afternoon. If you're going to stay here for a while you're going to have to work. You're going to have no time for running after strange men.'

'Oh, okay. I'll leave it be.' Lenore turned back into the room, took off her jacket and hung it up again.

They sat together at the round maplewood table that was set in the embrasure of the bow-shaped window overlooking the garden at the back of the inn. Not long free of the heaps of snow that had been dumped on that corner of the state of Maine during the winter, the grass was still brown and lifeless-looking, but in the flower-beds spears of yellow and purple crocuses were showing, harbingers of spring.

'The wind is still cold,' said Lenore. 'That bright sunshine is deceptive. How many guests are you expecting this weekend?'

'Three double rooms are booked, but we might have some others, especially if the sun keeps shining. It's Easter, remember, and lots of the townspeople like to drive down here at this time to visit the boatyard to check up on their boats after the winter and maybe even to start work on them. Here, have another doughnut. You're so thin you look as if you're suffering from anorexia nervosa.' Blythe frowned anxiously. 'I hope you're not. Mother wouldn't approve of the way you look at all.'

'Well, she isn't here to disapprove, is she?' retorted Lenore lightly. 'Have you heard from her lately?'

'I had a letter last week. She's coming here later in the year, maybe in July. Does she know about you and Herzel breaking up?'

'No, I haven't told her. I . . . I, oh, heck, I didn't want her telling me she told me so when I first started going with him.'

'What did she say?'

'She said it wouldn't last.'

'Did she give any reasons?'

'Several.' Lenore grimaced. 'The two most important were right.'

'What were they?'

'She said Herzel's religion would eventually come between us. He's an orthodox Jew and his parents apparently didn't approve of him going about with me, told him that if he married me he'd be cut off from his family. He asked me to convert. I refused, and so we agreed to part.'

'What was the other reason?' asked her sister.

'Mom said it isn't a good thing to marry or have a romance with someone in the same line of business or career, because there's always a danger of one becoming jealous of the other's success.' Lenore sighed. 'She was right again. Towards the end of the tour the orchestra did, the music director began to give me most of the clarinet solos to play, and Herzel was furious! When we got back to New York he quit the orchestra and went off to Israel. And I . . . well, you know the rest. I caught 'flu, it developed into pneumonia and I had to quit my job too.'

'And that's why you're here, to get better,' said Blythe comfortingly. 'More coffee?'

'No, thanks.'

'Then another doughnut.' Blythe pushed the plate of gold-brown sugared rings towards her sister. 'So your great love affair has ended,' she remarked with a touch of mockery. 'Hardly a good reason for starving yourself or to go into a decline, you know.'

'But you don't understand. You can't possibly understand how much it hurts to be rejected after . . . after you've put your trust in someone, believed in him when he's said he loves you, when you've given him your heart . . . given him everything,' sighed Lenore. 'You can't possibly understand, because you've never been in love.'

'Haven't I?' Blythe's round dark brown eyes gleamed with amusement. 'How do you know I haven't?'

'Well, you never seem to have been. You've

never gone steady with a man, to my knowledge, and you've always been more interested in your career, in working hard to save up to buy your own hotel.'

'That's true,' conceded Blythe. 'Learning to be a good chef and a good manager has always been more important to me than any man has, and I guess I've never known one I wanted to go steady with. How long have you been going with Herzel?'

'Nearly four years,' said Lenore, and groaned. 'When I think of it I could spit!' she went on. 'Four years of my life wasted, thinking he loved me and would one day marry me. Four years of being faithful to him, ever since I was twenty-two. It wouldn't be so bad if ... if *I* could have walked out on *him*. It's being rejected after giving so much that hurts, Blythe.'

'Forget him. No man is worth getting into the state you've got into. Put him right out of your mind.'

'I'm trying—I'm trying very hard,' whispered Lenore, looking quickly out of the window. 'Oh, look, there's a robin!' She watched the red-breasted bird tilt its head towards the soggy grass and listen intently, then start to poke fiercely at the turf with its long beak. 'That means no matter how cold the wind is spring is really on its way, doesn't it?'

'Spring and the promise of new life, the message of Easter,' murmured Blythe softly, her brown eyes soft as they considered the finely chiselled profile of her sister. 'A message for you, Lenore,' she added comfortingly. 'You'll get over it, and before you know where you are you'll be in love again, head over heels, because you're like that. You can't help loving.' Her manner changing, the brisk businesslike yet thoroughly charming hotel owner-manager taking over from the kindly elder sister, as she got to her feet. 'Now come on, time is going by and I want to make the desserts.'

'What are you going to give them tonight?' asked Lenore, wiping the tears from her eyes with the back of her hand and picking up the empty coffee mugs, banishing sentiment.

'Well, blueberry pie and fresh cream is always popular and I still have some of last year's blueberries in the freezer, but I also like to provide something a little exotic at this time of the year, something expressive of warm sunshine, of summer, so I'll make my own fruit cheesecake. We'll use those strawberries from Florida and canteloupe melon balls—you can make the balls with the special scoop I have—and something else with a warm colour, peaches, I think. Unfortunately they'll have to come out of a can. We'll decorate the centre with kiwi fruit. How does that sound?'

'Delicious,' said Lenore admiringly. 'You really are an artist, Blythe.'

'Well, so are you,' retorted Blythe, bending to take out cooking utensils from the cupboard. 'And that reminds me—on Sunday, at the brunch we serve, I'll introduce one of Northport's most respected celebrities, Isaac Goldstein. Ever heard of him?'

'You don't mean Isaac Goldstein the violinist?' gasped Lenore. 'What's he doing in Northport?'

'Living here. He retired a year ago and came to

live in one of the historic houses on Bay Street
East. There are a number of professional
musicians living in the area, some of them
teaching school music in Ellsworth and Bangor,
and Isaac already has them meeting regularly at
his house to practise and perform together. In
fact he's thinking of putting on a concert soon, if
he can find a suitable hall. When he meets you
he might invite you to join his music group.'

'I guess they're all string players,' said Lenore.

'No. Jack Kanata plays the piano.'

'Kanata—sounds Japanese.'

'It is, but Jack was born in the States, in
California. And Willa Caplan plays the viola.
She's from England by way of Canada and is the
wife of Fred Caplan who owns the local antique
store and art gallery. And I believe there's a
member who plays the bassoon.' Blythe smiled at
Lenore. 'I'm willing to bet you'll fit right in with
that crowd. Now, let me show you how to make
the melon balls.'

The first of the weekend guests arrived promptly
at three in the afternoon. They were a middle-
aged couple from Brooklyn, New York. In the
pleasant long living-room/lounge that was furnished with comfortable couches and armchairs
all covered in rose-pink slip covers, an antique
roll-topped desk, several bookcases and side
tables, Blythe greeted the couple just as if she was
welcoming them into her own home, then
introduced them to Lenore, who led them up the
stairs to the second floor.

The room she took them to was typical of the
inn. Not too big because part of it had been

partitioned off to make a private bathroom, it was furnished simply with two chests of drawers made from maplewood, a reproduction four-poster bed covered with a patchwork quilt handmade locally, and an old-fashioned ward-robe. Woven rugs were scattered about the shining oak floor and a rocking chair with cushions tied to its spindled back and its seat had been set by the window that, framed by flower-patterned curtains, overlooked the garden at the back of the inn, over the roofs of the houses further down the hill to the blue sun-glinting water of the estuary. Everything that could be done to preserve the early nineteenth-century look of the rooms had been done, at the same time providing every modern convenience includ-ing central heating and a hot water system.

When Lenore returned to the living room she found Blythe greeting the next couple to arrive, and from then on, for the rest of the afternoon she was busy showing people to their rooms because, as Blythe had predicted, the sunny weather had brought many visitors into the village and some had decided to stay overnight. At dinner-time she helped Carrie Carter, the young woman employed by Blythe both as a waitress and a housemaid, to wait on the more than twenty guests who had reserved tables for dinner, and afterwards she helped Blythe to clean up in the kitchen, rinsing dirty dishes and stacking them into the dishwasher, scouring cooking pans and also preparing for breakfast the next morning.

For the next three days she had little time to dwell on her own problems as she rushed from job to job, carrying out Blythe's calmly uttered instructions to the best of her ability, falling into bed in her small room in the attic to sleep dreamlessly, awakening early each morning to the sound of her sister's voice urging her to wake up and get with it because they had to serve several breakfasts.

On Sunday the routine changed slightly. Only coffee and muffins were available for early risers who wanted to go to one of the churches to attend the Easter Day services, because the main meal of the day was brunch, served from eleven o'clock onwards, buffet style, in the long sunlit dining room with its round tables and Windsor-style chairs. Not having to wait on tables, Lenore had time to talk to Isaac Goldstein, to whom Blythe introduced her as 'my musical sister'.

A silver-haired, swarthy-skinned man of about seventy years of age with twinkling black eyes set under bristling black eyebrows, the well-known violinist had brought his wife and his daughter who was visiting her parents, to brunch, as well as a young man with straight black hair and a definite Oriental slant to his dark eyes and a wide white smile.

'Jack is our conductor as well as being a fine pianist. He keeps us in order, disciplines us,' said Isaac. His accent was still thick and guttural, betraying his German origins, although he had lived in the States for many years.

'Are you staying in Northport for long, Lenore?' asked Jack.

'I haven't decided how long I'll stay,' she replied. 'As long as Blythe can bear with me, I guess.'

'You're not with an orchestra, then?'

'I was playing with one, but I had to quit when we returned from a tour of the country a few weeks ago. I developed pneumonia and I'm resting just now. Though helping Blythe in this inn for the past few days has hardly been a rest. We've really been busy.'

'You must come and play with us,' said Isaac. 'Next Thursday at seven at my house. So far we've been limited in what we can offer the public. At the moment we're looking for a cellist. You don't know one, do you?'

'Not living here,' replied Lenore. 'But thanks for the invitation. I'll look forward to Thursday.'

The guests who had been staying at the inn all departed next morning after breakfast and the old inn was quiet again. The weather had changed. Heavy grey clouds screened the sun and there was a strong wind. Seagulls blown in from the sea swooped and screamed above the rooftops and some circled down to perch on the guttering.

'A sign of bad weather to come,' said Blythe, pointing to the birds. 'And the forecast is for snow. I'm glad it held off until the weekend was over.'

'I think I'll go for a walk, then, before it comes,' announced Lenore, removing the apron she had been wearing. 'That is if you don't need me for anything?'

'No. We won't have any more guests until next weekend and I'm not serving dinners tonight. You go for your walk.'

'Like to come with me?' asked Lenore.

'No, thanks. I've got a date this afternoon,' replied Blythe, her dark eyes twinkling with mockery as she noticed Lenore's sharp enquiring glance in her direction.

'Here?' Although curiosity was bubbling up in Lenore she knew better than to question her sister too closely. Blythe was a very private person, not given to shouting about her affairs from the housetops.

'Yes, here. He's coming with the plans he's drawn up for an extension I'm thinking of having built on to the end of the dining room. It will be a sort of bar-lounge where people can sit and have cocktails while waiting for dinner to be served. I've already applied for a wine and spirit licence and have every hope of getting it.'

'Oh, you're expecting the architect to come,' murmured Lenore, her interest subsiding almost as quickly as it had bubbled up.'

'Well, yes, he is a kind of architect,' replied Blythe. 'He's Josh Kyd, and he owns the boatyard, designs and builds beautiful wooden boats.' Blythe looked around her gleaming kitchen at the smooth wooden counter tops, the wooden panelling against which copper pans gleamed. 'He designed and helped build this kitchen for me when things were slow at the boatyard this past winter,' she said, and there was pride in her glance and in her voice, arousing Lenore's interest again.

'Then I guess you're looking forward to seeing his plans for the dining room annexe as well as seeing him,' she remarked, and now her amber eyes held a glint of affectionate mockery. 'I promise to keep out of your way for a couple of hours. See you later.'

Dressed warmly in jeans and boots, a quilted

down-filled parka, a brightly coloured knitted cap pulled down over her ears and matching mittens on her hands, Lenore strode down Main Street and turned right into Bay Street West.

The street was narrow and without sidewalks, and followed the curving shoreline of the wide river estuary. On either side there were old clapboard houses, no two exactly alike. The first house had a brass plaque on its wall showing that it was of historical interest. Three storeys high, it had been built in 1800 for a doctor who had fought against the British in the American Revolution. There was a fine fan-shaped window over the solid front door.

On the other side of the street was a smaller house, known locally as 'the house of sin' because the original owner had broken the Sabbath by working on Sundays building ships. Behind the house was the boatyard, spiky with yacht masts. A man came out of the front door. Dressed in the ubiquitous jeans and quilted parka, he had a roll of paper under one arm. About forty years of age, he was lean and his uncovered wavy hair was grey.

He nodded in a friendly way to Lenore and walked off in the direction of Main Street. Watching him over her shoulder, Lenore guessed he was Josh Kyd, on his way to see Blythe.

She was glad Blythe had found a friend, she thought as she stepped out more briskly along the road. The wind sweeping in from the sea was raw, stinging her face. Above, the branches of tall elms creaked as they swayed, but the wide sturdy trunks of the trees didn't move. Many years old, amazingly free from the dreaded disease that had attacked so many of New England's elm trees, they seemed to be as solid as iron.

Now she was passing the Episcopal Church, built of stone in the Gothic style, on the corner of Bay Street and Leggatt Lane; its stained glass windows glinted blue-red and gold and its oak doors were closed. How often she had attended Sunday morning services there in the summertime when staying in Northport with her parents. They had always stayed in one of the cottages facing the estuary on Bay Street East, renting it from the owner—a Mrs Mather, a wealthy widow, who had lived in one of the big houses near the Golf Club.

How long since she had last walked this way? Lenore calculated backwards. Almost eight years ago, that last vacation she had spent with her parents, when she had been eighteen and had just graduated from High School and had been planning to go to New York to study music there. Eight years of her life that had gone by so quickly she had hardly noticed them passing. Eight years of dedication to her chosen career to be as good a musician as her father had been.

Her lips quivered and tears filled her eyes as she remembered her beloved father, Joe Parini. A lively but sensitive man, descended from Italian immigrants, he had died a little over three years ago from cancer. She had received her first music lessons from him, learning to play a soprano recorder at the age of five. He had himself played in the woodwind section of an orchestra for many years and he would have been pleased with her success as a clarinettist. Oh, how much she missed him!

Perhaps that was why she had turned to Herzel
Rubin for emotional support and musical advice.
A teacher of woodwind instruments at the music
college she had attended, he had suggested she
audition for an orchestra in which he had been
the leader of the woodwind section. She had been
appointed and they had become constant companions. Against her practical mother's advice
Lenore had moved into and had shared Herzel's
apartment to live with him freely, believing he
had loved her as she had loved him.

Oh, damn! She didn't want to think about
Herzel. She had come to stay in a place where he
had never been and that held only happy
memories of long serene summers; a place that
was renowned for peace and quiet, where people
could relax and forget about the rat-race of the
big cities; a place where the local inhabitants
never hurried, were slow-spoken and content to
carry on in the way of life of their forefathers,
working the land, fishing the sea, harvesting the
trees from the forests, building and repairing
fishing boats as well as fine yachts.

Past the oldest house in the village she walked,
a simple two-storey building set at right angles to
the wild wind-tossed grey waters of the estuary.
Old apple trees with twisted branches stood in its
back yard. Known as William Pickering's house,
it had been built as long ago as 1664 by one of
the original English settlers to come to what had
then been known as the Commonwealth of
Massachusetts. Beyond it were grass-covered
irregularly shaped mounds, all that remained of
an old fort that had been built by French settlers.

Past the brick-built museum where many

Indian artifacts were housed, together with old guns and muskets, relics of the many battles fought in the area; past some more grass-covered mounds, the foundations of another fort, built after the Revolution.

The road took a sudden turn to the right away from the estuary. A pathway slanted off the road to the left and curved over a hill. A signpost bore the words Pickering Point Lighthouse.

Leaning against the wind, Lenore fought her way along the path, intending to walk as far as the old lighthouse, long abandoned in favour of an automatic beacon set at the foot of the sheer cliffs of Pickering Point. Soon she could see the cylindrical tower with its black-painted pointed top where the light had once been contained, rearing up starkly against the sky across which dark grey snow-laden clouds were being pushed by the wind.

Snow began to fly. In a few seconds the soggy winter-brown grass was covered white. The wood of pine trees to her right rustled and sighed as the wind whipped through them. Time to turn back before she was caught in a blizzard, thought Lenore, but she kept on, determined to have at least one glimpse of the sea raging against the rocks at the foot of the cliffs.

Battered by the wind, her cheeks stung red by icy snowflakes, she reached the edge of the cliffs and looked across the wide bay. No sign of islands or of the distant Camden Hills. They were all hidden in the snowy murk, and below her the foghorn sounded its dismal wail. She saw the surf leaping and crashing against dark primeval rocks, and then, feeling the cold

penetrating her jacket, she turned and began to
hurry back along the path, driven by the wind,
her back soon coated with snow.

It would be quicker to go through the woods
and back to the road, she decided. Often in the
past she had taken that route across the Jonson
land, and now she didn't hesitate to duck under
what looked like new fencing to gain shelter
under the dark plumes of the pines.

But where there had once been a path clearly
marked there was only a tangle of undergrowth and
fallen trees through which she had to force her way,
changing course several times until she was
completely disorientated, not knowing if she was
going towards the road or back towards the
windswept headland. Above, the tree branches
creaked and groaned. At eye-level other branches
protruded, snatching at her parka, scratching her
cheeks and even sometimes attacking her eyes. She
seemed to be trapped in a gloomy green nightmare,
tripping over hidden rocks and fallen tree trunks,
wishing she had never decided to come that way,
remembering stories she had heard of the dangers
of walking in the winter woods and how sometimes
people had been lost in them for ever.

At last she saw space between tree trunks; a
space filled with sideways-slanting snowflakes.
She made towards it and found she was on the
edge of the wood at last, looking across a field
covered with snow towards the shape of a house
with pointed gables and a turret at one corner.
Dark grey, it looked darker than the trees and
clouds behind it, veiled by snow, somehow
ghostly and forbidding. No light twinkled from
any of its windows.

She was far away from the road, she realised. Instead of bearing right through the woods as she had thought she had been doing, she had cut straight through them. But she wasn't going back into them. She would walk right across the field to the driveway of the house which she could just see, a double row of pine trees. It would lead her into the road and she would be able to follow Pickering Lane to Main Street, coming out uphill from the Inn.

The wind whined and the snow lashed at her as she crossed the field, which was exposed to the west and the sea. No one in their right mind would be out of doors in this weather, she thought wryly, not even the tough guy who lived in the old house. As Blythe had said, it was a godforsaken place to live in—and yet looking back to her childhood she could remember seeing it bathed in golden sunshine, its clapboard gleaming, its windows brimming with reflected light. She could remember too this field, starred with wild flowers, its long grass shimmering green and gold under a light summer breeze. Then the old house had seemed to her to be a fairy castle in which a beautiful princess might have lived. Now it seemed like a derelict ruin in which a monster lurked.

Laughing at her gothic fantasy, Lenore tripped over a snow-covered rock and went sprawling on the ground, banging her right knee on another unseen rock. Pain from the bruised kneecap zig-zagged through her leg making her gasp when she kneeled on it before standing up. Slowly she bent the leg again. More pain. Somehow she managed to get to her feet and looked around to get her bearings, then she began to limp onwards in the direction of the line of trees edging the driveway. Her bruised knee twinged painfully and it took all her grit and determination to keep going.

At last, gasping for breath, having fallen several times, she reached the driveway. Leaning against the trunk of one of the pine trees, she felt her right knee through the thick denim of her jeans. There was a lump like an egg on the knee-cap and when she pressed with her fingers the pain was excruciatingly sharp.

She looked down the driveway. It seemed to wind off into an infinity of wildly dancing snowflakes. It seemed to be miles long, going nowhere and soon to disappear under high drifts of snow being blown across it. And Pickering Lane would be even longer. It would take her hours to reach the Inn with her knee in this painful state, and she was afraid she might damage it permanently if she walked too far while it was hurting.

Of course, she would probably get assistance from the first house she reached in Pickering Lane, but the Jonson house was nearer. She turned her head and looked at it. Dark and high, it loomed close at hand. A few limping strides and she would be at the foot of its steps. A few more and she would be on the wide covered verandah and could knock on the door.

Pushing away from the tree, she began to limp towards the house, but the short time she had been resting it her right leg had grown stiff and somehow useless. She lost her balance again and fell down in a heap of soft snow, and wondered if she would ever get up again.

The wind howled in the tree-tops, the snowflakes whirled across the land. Soon she would be covered. She would be *buried* in snow! The thought was enough to make her get up and reach the house.

Limping and hopping she went, climbed the steps on all fours, and collapsed on the verandah floor in front of the elegant front door with its spiderweb transom and brass knocker and knob. Dragging herself across to the door, she thumped on the lower panels with a clenched fist.

Nothing happened, so she thumped harder, several times, and then listened. She thought she could hear a dog barking, so she thumped again.

After a while—it seemed like hours—the door swung open slowly and faint yellow light slanted out. Lenore looked up. Adam Jonson stood in the doorway, his light-coloured hair shining under the yellow light, his dark glasses glinting as he peered down at her. Beside him sat a dog, a beautifully arrogant, well-kept German Shepherd, wearing a guide-dog harness.

CHAPTER TWO

THE dog growled softly and bared its teeth.

'Shut up, Caesar!' ordered Adam Jonson, and peered out into the darkness of the verandah. 'Is anyone there?' he demanded roughly. 'Who's there?'

'It ... it's me,' croaked Lenore. 'I ... I'm Lenore Parini and ... oh, please don't close the door! Don't go away. *Please!* I ... I've hurt my knee and I can't walk very well. Please, Mr Jonson, can I come in and use your phone?'

Slowly, reluctantly, the door swung wide again and he stepped out.

'What are you doing here?' he asked.

'I ... I've been for a walk as far as the lighthouse, and coming back, since it was snowing hard, I thought I'd take the short cut through the woods to the road,' she explained, still sitting on the floor and looking up at him. In the faint light coming from the hallway the cream-coloured wool of his Aran-style sweater gleamed softly. But he seemed huge to her, a giant living in the derelict ruin of her gothic fantasy.

'You were trespassing,' he accused. 'You have no right to come this way. Why didn't you keep to the public pathway?'

'I couldn't find it, that's why,' she retorted. 'The woods are a mess now, with fallen trees and tangled undergrowth. I was lucky to find my way out of them. They used to be beautiful when Martin Jonson was alive. *He* knew how to take care of his land!'

He let her caustic and critical remarks go straight past him and continued to stare down at her as if trying to see her.

'You're the woman who walked into me outside the supermarket, aren't you?' he drawled.

'Yes, I am. And I've wanted to say I'm sorry about that,' she said, forgetful of Blythe's warning about him being proud and touchy about his incapacity. 'You see, I didn't know that . . . that you can't see too well or I wouldn't have said what I did.'

'Who told you I don't see too well?' he rapped.

'My sister Blythe did—she owns the Northport Inn. On the other hand,' she went on, refusing to be intimidated by the hint of menace in his attitude, 'you had no right to swear at me the way you did that day.'

He said nothing but went on staring at her, seemingly finding nothing strange about the situation, her lying on the floor at his feet and, beyond the verandah, the snow swirling, the wind howling.

'Oh, this is crazy,' Lenore muttered. 'Please let me come in and use your phone to call my sister and ask her to drive out here and pick me up. I can't possibly walk all the way back to the Inn. My knee is very swollen and I'm afraid of damaging it if I go on.'

'Which knee?' he demanded, advancing on her.

'The right one,' she whispered, sensing a threat in the way he approached her but unable to move away.

He squatted suddenly beside her and his big hands reached out searchingly, touched her thighs and slid over them. Surprised and alarmed by his touch, Lenore stiffened all over. His hands stopped moving and he turned his head as if to look at her, his lips thinning in exasperation, his jaw taut.

'Okay, okay, take it easy. I've nothing else in mind right now except to make sure your knee really is swollen before I let you into my house,' he drawled. 'Not being able to see too well, I'm suspicious of strangers—particularly women. Since I was blinded more than one has tried to take advantage of me.'

'Well, I'm not like that,' retorted Lenore, seething with fury. 'Oh, I wish I'd never come this way ... aah!' she cried out as, ignoring her protest, he found her right knee and pressed the swelling.

'Mmm, it does seem swollen,' he murmured. 'Okay, you can come in and make your phone call.'

Standing up straight, he held out a hand to her. Lenore grasped it and managed to stand up. Then suddenly without warning his arms went about her and he lifted her as easily as if she had been made of straw and carried her into the house.

'Please put me down,' she said rather weakly, while secretly admitting to herself that she was enjoying being carried in such a masterful way.

Ignoring her again, he carried her across a high-ceilinged dimly lit panelled hallway into a big room, with three long windows through which grey light slanted, and set her down on an enormous high-backed, brocade-covered sofa that was set at right angles to a cavernous fireplace where a log fire blazed.

'I suggest you put your legs up,' he said coolly. 'It won't do your knee any good sitting with it bent. I'll get you the phone.'

He walked away from her out of her sight and she did what he had suggested, stretching her legs along the cushioned sofa and thinking she should really take off her boots. She was unzipping them when he returned with the phone. He plugged it into a jack near the fireplace, then set the instrument down on the dust-filmed newspaper and magazine-cluttered long coffee table that was beside the sofa. Then he went away again, through the doorway into the hall, the dog padding at his heels, and as she drew off her boots she heard him shutting the front door.

Picking up the phone, she rested it on her thighs and lifting the receiver held it to her ear. There didn't seem to be any dialling tone, but she dialled the number of the Inn anyway. There were some clicking sounds followed by a swishing sound. Replacing the receiver, she waited a moment, then lifted it again. No dialling tone.

Adam Jonson came back into the room.

'Your phone seems to be out of order. There's no dialling tone,' she said.

'Did you dial the number you want?' he asked, pushing aside some of the clutter on the table and sitting down on it right opposite to her so that he was on a level with her.

'Yes, but nothing happened. Here.' She handed him the instrument and his hands found it unerringly. He could see it, that was obvious, but then he was very close to it and to her.

'It was okay this morning when I made a call to Boston,' he muttered, frowning. He lifted the receiver and listened to it. 'What number do you want?'

She told him, and watched him dial with a big blunt-ended forefinger. Again he didn't hesitate. He could see what he was doing. After a few moments he set the receiver down on its rest and put the phone down on the table.

'You're right—it's out of order. The wind must have brought the wires down. We had this trouble in the winter.' The dark glasses were staring at her face. 'So what now?'

'Do you have a car?' she asked hopefully.

'No. What would be the use of a car to me? I can't see well enough to get a driving licence.'

'Not even with glasses on?'

'Not even with glasses on,' he repeated dryly.

'But you walked into the house and into this room as if you could see where you were going, and just now you dialled as if you could see the numbers,' she remarked suspiciously.

'I can walk into and out of the house, I can walk about it because it's familiar territory,' he replied. 'And I can see things if I'm close to them.'

'How close? Can you see me now?'

'Sure I can. I can see the shape of your face, where your eyes are and where your mouth is.' He leaned towards her so near to her that through the dark brown lenses of the glasses she could see the shape of his eyes, the gleam of their whites; so near she could see the golden blur of bristles on his square jaw and above the shapely curve of his long upper lip and under the bristles tiny scars as if the skin had been cut and sewn up again. Yet in spite of the scars, the bristles and the untidiness of his hair, drying now and beginning to glint with golden lights, he was handsome in a rough-hewn way. 'Your eyes are golden-brown and they're big and round and wide open and looking at me very suspiciously,' he murmured softly. His lips tilted in a faint tantalising smile. 'You're not bad looking, but you'd be better looking if your face wasn't so haggard.'

'It's not haggard!' she flared, moving away from him and leaning back against the high back of the sofa. He could see too much, she decided.

'Okay. Fashionably hollow-cheeked, then.' His smile widened into a wide white grin and she felt her heart do a funny little flip as she reluctantly acknowledged that she was physically attracted to him. Strange, because she had never been attracted by the rugged outdoor type of man before. She had always been more interested in the cultured type of man; in the mind rather than in the actual outward appearance. 'Like most women, you don't care to be told the truth about how you look,' he added jibingly, with a cynical twist to his lips.

'Well, how would you like it if . . . if I told you the truth about how you look right now?' she retorted spiritedly. 'With your hair unbrushed, a day's growth of beard on your face and with those dark glasses you look . . . well, you look disreputable and dissipated.'

'Ha!' Again his short gruff laugh disconcerted her. 'A woman of spirit, with a good command of language.' His face hardened. The curve to his lips was bitter. 'I am disreputable and dissipated,' he drawled. 'I've been drinking too much rye whisky.'

'Sorry for yourself?' Lenore couldn't help taunting, although she was surprised that he would indulge in self-pity.

'You bet I am,' he replied shortly. 'You would be too if you'd been told that your eyesight isn't going to get any better than it is and that you might as well give up all hope of ever seeing well enough to do the things you like doing!' His voice rasped harshly. 'And that there'll always be days when you'll walk into people ... or objects because you don't see them.'

'Who told you that?' Lenore whispered, feeling sympathy for him uncoiling within her. Big and obviously strong—she remembered how easily he had carried her—he had probably led a very physical life before he had been hurt and blinded, and now, having recovered his strength, he was suffering from frustration.

'An ophthalmic surgeon, one of the best.'

'When did he tell you?'

'Last week, in New York. I went there for a check-up.'

'But lots of people who are blind—really blind, I mean—are able to lead useful and productive lives. Some of them have even become well-known performers.'

'Performers?' he queried, frowning in puzzlement.

'I was thinking of George Shearing the jazz pianist. And then there's Stevie Wonder,' she said.

'Both musicians. They don't have to be able to see to do what they like doing,' he said dryly. 'I do. I have to be able to see to use a camera.'

'You're a photographer?'

'Cameraman. TV,' he said curtly. 'I worked for a national broadcasting corporation—overseas news. Frank Carson and I were reporting on the fighting in a Central American country—actually covering a street battle between guerillas and government forces—when someone took exception to our presence there and threw a hand grenade right at us. Frank was killed.' He broke off, his lips twisting bitterly again. 'I wish to God I had been,' he added in a low voice, and lunging to his feet he walked round the end of the table and over to the winged chair. With his back to Lenore he picked up the half-full glass on the occasional table and drank off the liquor that was in it.

'When? When did it happen?' whispered Lenore, her sensitive soul seared by what he had just told her. Violence of any sort always appalled her.

'Must be about two years ago,' he replied indifferently, shrugging his broad shoulders. He poured more whisky into the glass and sat down in the armchair, facing her, although she supposed he couldn't see her very well, because the room was growing dim now as daylight faded completely. 'Since then I've been fighting to come back to life,' he continued dryly. 'Learning to stand, learning to walk. All of it wasted effort.' He hit the arm of the chair with one fist and swore bitterly. Both Lenore and the dog were startled by his movement and by the bitter harshness of his voice, and they both jumped. The dog, which had been lying on the rug in front of the fire, sat up straight, its ears quivering, its head tilted to one side as it looked at its master. 'What earthly good am I if I can't see to do what I want to do?' grated Adam Jonson, and drank more whisky.

'Isn't that a rather defeatist attitude to take?' asked Lenore, sharply for her, aware of compassion for him flooding through her but wanting to hide it as she realised he would only reject any show of pity on her part.

'And what other attitude do you suggest I should take?' he replied jeeringly. 'You can't even begin to understand how I feel.'

'I can guess,' she retorted.

He was silent, and the room grew darker, the only light being the orange blaze of the fire. Music—she recognised it as a guitar concerto by the Brazilian composer Villa-Lobos—came faintly from a radio which she guessed was on the bookshelves built into the wall on one side of the fireplace behind the winged chair.

The logs crackled as they were consumed by flames. The wind moaned eerily in the chimney. Lenore shifted uneasily. Adam Jonson's silence was unnerving and he seemed to have forgotten she was there. Next minute she jumped nervously when he spoke suddenly.

'Is your name really Lenore?'

'Would I say it was if it wasn't?' she countered lightly.

'I guess not. It's not a common name,' he murmured, and there was another short silence. Then: 'Lenore,' he said again, his voice deep yet strangely resonant. '"*A dirge for her, the doubly dead*,"' he continued softly, and she felt the hairs prick the back of her neck. '"*In that she died so young.*" You know Edgar Allan Poe's poem entitled *Lenore*?' he added.

'No, I don't.'

'That's all I can remember of the poem. He seemed to have had a fixation about a woman of that name, because she appears in another of his poems *The Raven*. Surely you know that one?'

'No, I . . . I don't think so.'

'The way you came here this evening reminded me of it, even though it's a different time of day. This house, its remoteness and the wildness of the weather right now would have appealed to Edgar Allan. Could be he was in a similar situation when he wrote the poem. Listen:

"Once upon a midnight dreary, while I pondered weak and weary,

Over many a quaint and curious volume of forgotten lore,

While I nodded nearly napping, suddenly there came a tapping,

As of someone gently rapping."'

He stopped quoting and laughed softly, and again Lenore felt a shiver go down her spine.

'When you knocked on the door I was sitting here, half asleep by the fire,' he said, 'so I went to the door and,

"Deep into the darkness peering, long I stood there wondering, fearing,

Doubting, dreaming dreams no mortal ever dared to dream. . . ."'

'Oh, stop it!' exclaimed Lenore. 'Stop trying to scare me!' She swung her legs off the sofa, found her boots and began to pull them on.

'What are you doing?' he demanded sharply.

'Putting on my boots.' Groping, she found her woollen hat and crammed it down on her head, then zipped up her parka and pulling on her wet mitts she stood up, putting all her weight on her left leg. 'I . . . I . . . my knee feels much better now, so I think I'll try to get to Pickering Lane and the first house and phone my sister from there. She must be getting anxious about me. Thank you for letting me stay and rest for a while.'

She began to limp towards the doorway and the dimly lit hall, wincing at every step. Behind her she heard Adam say something, then heard him coming after her. By the time she reached the door he was beside her and the dog was with him.

'Don't be a fool,' he said autocratically, stepping between her and the hall. 'You'll never make it to Pickering Lane in this blizzard—not now, not limping the way you are. You'll have to stay the night here.'

'But I don't want to stay the night. And you don't want me to stay,' she retorted. 'Not really. You didn't want me to come into the house and you've just done your best to scare me away. You don't want me here, so I'll leave.'

She stepped sideways to go around him and towards the door, but somehow the dog was under her feet. Lurching wildly, she went crashing down on the floor, banging her right knee again, this time against the hard oak frame of the doorway. The pain was sharp, excruciating, and she cried out gaspingly. The dog growled at her fiercely.

'What the hell?' exclaimed Adam Jonson. 'Lenore, where are you?'

'Here on the floor, by the living room door,' she moaned. 'I . . . I tripped over the dog and I've hurt my knee again. Oh, what am I going to do?'

He ordered the dog away from her and crouched down beside her. Again his hands reached out to her. His fingers brushed against her cheek, lingered for a moment as if they liked the feel of it before flinching away suddenly, curling into the palm of his hand as it balled into a fist.

'Have you no sense?' he snapped, his lips curving back from his set white teeth in the now familiar snarl. 'Are you always like this, taking offence and rushing off without thinking?'

He was so near to her that she felt the warmth of his breath on her face and smelt the tang of whisky on it. She could feel too the warmth of his body radiating out to her, heard the strong beat of his heart. Suddenly she felt an urge to touch his face as he had inadvertently touched hers, to run the tips of her fingers over the stubble of his beard, trace the line of his lips or raise her hand even higher and stroke back the fronds of dusty-blond hair from his brow.

Amazed at herself, because never before had she experienced such a spontaneous urge to reach out and touch a person, to offer the sort of comfort to a man that she knew only a woman could offer, she also clenched her hands as if preventing them from reaching out to him. 'Why?' she repeated huskily. 'Why did you want to stop me from leaving?'

He didn't answer right away but stared at her through the dark lenses. Then he shrugged and smiled rather twistedly.

'God knows,' he said. 'I guess you'll have to stay here for the night. You can't go out into that blizzard if you can't walk properly. You might fall down again and not be able to get up. Or you might get lost, and then there'd be hell to pay.'

'But my sister,' she argued. 'She's going to be so anxious when I don't return to the Inn.'

'Didn't you tell her which way you'd be walking?'

'No, I didn't.' She chewed at her lip. 'But she might guess. To the lighthouse and then back through the woods to Pickering Lane used to be one of our walks when we stayed in Northport with our parents. And Martin Jonson never objected to us using the path through the woods. He *never* sued anyone for trespassing.'

'Okay, I get the message,' he retorted. 'But he had advantages I don't have. He'd lived here all his life. I'm a stranger. Also he could see properly. Did you ever meet him?'

'Several times. He always used to speak to us when we met him the woods. He was a nice old gentleman, very polite.'

'And I'm not,' he conceded with a grin. 'How you love to score points!'

'Is it true?' she asked. 'Are you really a relative of his?'

'It's true, strange as it may seem to you,' he drawled. 'My grandfather, another Adam Jonson, was Martin's younger brother. Adam was a wild one, a bit of a rebel. He stole Martin's girl-friend and eloped with her. She was my grandmother.

The story goes that Martin was so hurt that he never married. But you must be uncomfortable sprawled on the floor the way you are. Here, let me help you up.'

He stood up straight and reached down both hands to her. Lenore grasped them and pulled herself up on to her feet. The movement brought her very close to him again, but when she would have freed her hands from his grasp, his fingers tightened. She looked up at him quickly and defensively. The dark glasses looked down at her.

The silent moment seemed to twang with electrifying awareness. Lenore had a strange feeling that she had stood with him or someone like him in this hallway before, had held hands with him, had looked up at him and had waited with the same pulse-quickening anticipation for his next move.

'Are you like your grandfather, the other Adam Jonson?' she whispered.

'I don't know—I never met him,' he replied. 'Why do you ask?'

Some sixth sense was warning her to step back, to pull her hands from his, but she didn't move. *She couldn't move.* She was caught and held in some kind of spell. She was spellbound by this blond ruffian, by the warm grasp of his hands, by the movement of his shapely lips as they parted. In the next instant they were touching hers.

Finding no resistance in her, his lips moved experimentally, exploring the softness of hers. Mistakenly believing she was sufficiently worldly-wise to let him kiss her and remain unmoved, Lenore was unprepared for what happened next. Response surged through her, springing up from the deep well of emotions that had been frozen over since she had parted from Herzel, and answering instinctively the desperate hunger expressed by Adam's hard warm lips.

Impulsively she lifted her hands to his face to caress the lean scarred cheeks. She stroked her lips, warm and generous, quivering with passion, against his. She swayed against him and his arms went around her, strong as iron, locking her softness against his hardness. For a few sense-inflaming, mind-reeling moments they seemed to be fused together by the heat of mutual physical desire that blazed up between them and, like wildfire, destroyed all the defences each of them had built up over the years to protect themselves against such an assault.

The kiss ended as abruptly as it had begun. Adam lifted his mouth from hers and his arms dropped to his sides. Her hands slid away from his cheeks, yet still the spell held and they continued to stare at each other in a bemused silence, oblivious to the reality of the dimly lit hallway, the dog sitting and watching them, the creaks and groans of the old house as it withstood the battering of the spring storm.

It was Adam who broke the spell with a violent repudiating gesture of one hand. He broke the silence too, uttering a crisp ear-tingling oath which made Lenore flinch back from him.

'I knew something like this would happen if I let *you* into my house,' he growled. 'I've been too long without a woman, and the scents of your skin and hair, the feel of you, went to my head. Turned me on.' He laughed shortly, mirthlessly, his head going back, his lips curving tautly over his teeth. 'I suppose I should be glad that you did,' he added dryly. 'Proves I'm still normal in that area. I was beginning to wonder!'

As understanding of what he was saying dawned on Lenore; alarm jangled along her nerves and the last of the spell faded, completely destroyed by his harsh statement of the reality of the situation.

'Then let me go, let me leave!' she cried out wildly, and would have lurched past him towards the front door, but he caught hold of her by the shoulders with his big hands and held her still in front of him, and again she felt as lacking in bone and muscle as a doll stuffed with straw.

'I can't let you go—not now. You'll have to stay,' he grated through set teeth. He released her suddenly and she staggered back against the door frame, clutching at the sturdy oak with her hands, clinging to it as a wrecked sailor clings to a spar in storm-tossed seas, feeling as if she was indeed being tossed about on the tempest of Adam's anger and frustration.

'*God!*' he growled, one hand going to his head. 'Don't look at me like that! I'm not going to hurt you. What happened just now ... was a temporary aberration.' Thrusting his hands into his pants pockets, he made a visible effort to control his fury.

'Go and lie on the sofa again,' he suggested more quietly. 'You'll have to rest your leg.' He drew a sharp hissing breath and added, 'But you'll have to get there under your own steam, I'm sure as hell not going to carry you again. Go on, get moving!' He jerked his head towards the firelit room.

'I ... I ...' was all she could croak as she clung to the door frame and continued to stare at him with wide eyes.

'Go on!' he roared at her. 'You can't stand here all night.'

'Yes, I ... I will do what you say,' she whispered, 'but please would you put a light on in there? I ... I don't want to walk into anything and bang my knee again. And ... and please don't shout at me any more. I ... I can't bear to be shouted at.'

'Okay, okay.' He sounded thoroughly exasperated, but he went into the room and flicked a switch on the wall. 'There you are,' he said, coming back to her. 'Now you can see. Go and rest your leg and calm down. There's nothing to be nervous about. I've told you, I'm not going to touch you again. I'm going to the kitchen to fix us something to eat—it's way past supper time.'

He turned away from her, gave an order to the dog, which went to lie in front of the front door, then went across the hall and through another door that she guessed led to the kitchen.

Limping back into the big room, she was aware that two lights were on, a standard lamp behind the sofa and a lamp on the table beside the winged chair. Reaching the sofa, she sat down slowly, stretching her right leg before her. She took off her hat and mitts again, then unzipped her jacket and took that off. She put everything in a neat pile on one of the wide arms of the sofa, then easing herself into the corner by the other arm, she leaned back against it and swung her legs up.

Now she was alone reaction to what had

happened in the hallway was beginning to set in. Her breath expelling in a long shaky sigh, she closed her eyes. For a kiss between complete strangers it had been a shattering experience. Her cheeks grew hot at the memory of it, and blood was a bittersweet taste on her tongue. Opening her eyes, she touched her lower lip with a finger, than studied the fingertip. Yes, her lips had been cut by the sharpness of straight white teeth.

A temporary aberration on his part, Adam had called his behaviour, and she understood only too well what he had meant. A sexually experienced man who had just regained his full physical strength after having been seriously injured, he had been shaken momentarily out of his usual control by close contact with her.

But what about her own behaviour? Why had she kissed him back? Why had she lost control too? What had happened to those moral standards by which she had governed her personal life so far, one of the most important being never to kiss or make love with a man she wasn't in love with? She was supposed to be in love with Herzel, wasn't she, and she had told Blythe that she would never fall in love with a man again, after being rejected by him.

And she hadn't She hadn't fallen in love with Adam Jonson. She couldn't have—there hadn't been time. And anyway, most of what she knew about him she didn't like. He was a rude ruffian, a bully, who probably thought of himself as superior to women and who was sorry for himself because he could no longer project a macho image now that he knew his eyesight would never improve. Physically strong and attractive, following a potentially dangerous career as a TV foreign news cameraman, he had probably wowed many women in his time; the sort of women who liked being overwhelmed by brute force. Well, she wasn't one of them.

Then why had she kissed him back? Another 'temporary aberration'? A primitive need in her answering an equally primitive need in him? She groaned in dismay at the discovery that she could feel sexually attracted to a man she hardly knew and didn't love.

With the back of one hand against one hot cheek she closed her eyes and groaned again. But not only were her cheeks hot, her whole body seemed to be burning. Burning with shame? Because he must have noticed her response. He must have. Oh, if only she could leave without having to see him again! With one kiss he had managed to break through her poise, smashing it as if it had been an eggshell and exposing her for what she was, a woman who liked to love but who needed, oh, how desperately, to be loved in return.

She opened her eyes and looked towards the doorway, thinking she might leave while he was in the kitchen. But the idea had hardly flitted through her mind before she rejected it. She would never get past the dog. And then . . . did she really want to go out into the whirling snow to flounder about and fall, lose her way? No, she didn't want to leave this warm, peaceful haven, even if it was inhabited by a half-crazy, partly blind tough guy. She would have to stay the night and hope that Blythe would not be too anxious and that eventually, maybe tomorrow

when the storm had blown itself out, someone
would come looking for her and take her back to
the Inn.

CHAPTER THREE

WALKING slowly and carefully, carrying a tray laden with two steaming soup bowls and a basket of bread rolls, Adam Jonson came back into the room. While he approached the long table in front of the sofa Lenore sat up, swung her legs off the sofa and shuffled newspapers and magazines together to one end of the table, making room for the tray.

Adam set the tray down in the space she had provided and turning away took hold of the winged chair and drew it close to the other side of the table then sat down to face her.

'Bertha Smith's own special fish chowder and her home-baked rolls are all I can offer,' he said coolly. 'Help yourself.' He picked up the basket of rolls and held it towards her.

'Thank you. Thank you very much,' she whispered as she took one of the hot golden-brown crusty rolls, amazed that he should have gone to so much trouble for her. The tray was set with a white linen cloth on which stainless steel knives and spoons of the best quality gleamed. The soup bowls were thick heat-resistant blue pottery. No man had ever waited on her like this. Herzel had never done. In fact she doubted if Herzel could have produced a meal, even one as simple as this. 'Thank you,' she said again in awe-struck tones, 'for . . . for going to so much trouble.'

'You're welcome,' he replied automatically,

then added fiercely, dark glasses glaring at her, 'No, I take that back—you're not welcome here. Why couldn't you have walked somewhere else this afternoon? Why the hell did you have to come this way? Why didn't you fall down on someone else's land and ask to use his phone? The hell you're welcome here! Now, what's the matter? Don't you like chowder?'

'Yes, I do. It ... it's you I don't like,' she flared. 'And, and ... if ... if you weren't partly blind, I'd ... I'd hit you for being so rude to me, for swearing at me and for ... for ...' she broke off, almost choking on the anger that was gusting through her. Never, never had she been so angry. But then never in the whole of her gently-nurtured life had she been so abused. Always she had been surrounded by and had moved among polite, sensitive people, none of whom had ever spoken harshly to her or to each other; her parents, Blythe, other relatives, school friends, fellow musicians, Herzel. None of them had ever expressed violent emotions violently as this man did, presumably because they didn't experience violent emotions ...

'For kissing you?' The jeering abrasive voice cut through her chaotic rambling thoughts.

'Yes, that too,' she retorted, with dignity, picking up a spoon and dipping it into the thick, creamy chowder in which succulent pieces of lobster floated, exotically pink in the whiteness surrounding them.

'If you feel like hitting me never let my infirmity stop you,' he continued mockingly, tearing a roll apart with lean fingers. 'It isn't healthy to bottle up deeply felt emotions.'

'Is that why you let fly all the time?' she queried tauntingly.

'Right.' His quick grin came and went. He bit into the roll with sharp white teeth, chewed for a moment, then said in a completely different tone, softly and with just a suggestion of laughter shaking his voice, 'I'm not going to apologise, you know.'

'For what?'

'For my behaviour. In particular for kissing you. I enjoyed kissing you, and your way of kissing me back made it an experience to remember, to mull over during sleepless nights. You're certainly no innocent when it comes to kissing—you've been around.'

Lenore's cheeks flamed. There was a roaring in her ears. Before she realised it her right hand flicked out across the space between her and him and her fingers smacked sharply against his left cheek.

His head jerked back a little. Horrified by what she had done—never before had she hit anyone— Lenore snatched her hand back and shifted uneasily on the sofa, away from him, afraid he might retaliate in kind. But he only laughed.

'Now I know I was wrong in implying that you've slept around,' he drawled. 'You're no easy lady. But you're not innocent either when it comes to kissing and making love. You're not married—at least you don't wear a ring. I didn't feel one when I was holding your hands. Are you divorced?'

'No, I'm not. Oh, this is a silly conversation. Why should I tell you anything about myself?' she retorted.

'No reason why you should,' he replied equably. 'But if you don't I'll just have to go on making guesses, won't I? So you live at the Northport Inn. Are you in business with your sister?'

'No. I'm just staying with her for a while.'

'Unemployed?'

'Temporarily. I'm a musician—I play the clarinet. I've been playing with a symphony orchestra for the past three years, but this past month I came down with pneumonia, so I came here to recuperate.'

'You should have gone south to Florida or the Bahamas, somewhere where the sun shines,' he commented.

'I couldn't afford to go anywhere like that,' she replied evasively. 'Besides, I wanted to be somewhere quiet, where I knew there wouldn't be lots of people. I've always found Maine a good place to relax in. Why did you come here? Why didn't you go somewhere warmer to recuperate?'

'I came here because I had nowhere else to go when I left hospital—that is, nowhere where I was wanted.' His lips curled in a bitter grimace. 'And like you, I wanted to be alone too.'

'It took you a long time to come here. Martin Jonson died eight years ago, the last time I spent a vacation here with my parents.'

'It was a while before the executor of the will caught up with me to tell me I'd inherited the place.' Adam gave one of his short laughs. 'No one was more surprised than I was when I came back to the States from an assignment in the Middle East to find that a great-uncle I'd never even heard of had left his house and a large annuity of seventy thousand dollars to me because I'm apparently the only descendant of his brother and the woman he loved. That was about four years ago. I was going to come and see the place then, but was sent abroad again.' He paused, frowning. 'After being shattered by that hand-grenade I was in hospital for two years,' he added slowly. 'When I came out this seemed to be a good place to hole up in, lick my wounds and get my act together before going back to the crazy world of filming the more violent aspects of human behaviour. But I thought that by now I'd be able to see properly.' He hit the arm of the chair with a fist. 'Dammit, I should be able to see by now!' he grated through set teeth.

Picking up his spoon, he continued to eat his chowder. Lenore watched him, noting how he didn't spill a drop and aware of a longing building up inside her to reach out and comfort him in some way; to do things for him; to help him overcome his handicap.

'Six months,' he muttered, still speaking tautly. 'Six months, the specialists said when I left the hospital. That's what it would take, they said, for me to be able to see again. Six months of quiet and rest. Well, it's been quiet enough here—too quiet, sometimes. And I've rested—my God, how I've rested! I've never been so inactive in my life. Yet still I can't see well enough to walk through the village without walking into something or someone like ... like I walked into you.' Throwing down the spoon in his empty chowder bowl, he flung himself back in his chair. 'So it looks as if I'm going to be here for the rest of my life, rotting away, a useless hulk. . . .'

'No, oh, no,' she protested. 'It doesn't have to be like that. You'll find something useful to do.'

'What, for instance?' he asked dryly. 'What would you do if for some reason you weren't able to play your clarinet any more? What would you do if you'd lost your hearing and couldn't make music?'

'Naturally I'd be upset for a long time, but I wouldn't let myself rot. I'd find something to do. I'd probably take up some sort of visual art.' Lenore looked around the room, at the sheen on green velvet curtains hanging at long windows, at the gleam of the golden wood of antique furniture and finally at the magnificent rosewood grand piano that stood at the far end of the wide long room, behind Adam and beyond the doorway. 'I guess that piano is the one Martin Jonson used to play,' she mused aloud.

'I guess it is,' he drawled indifferently.

'My father once told me that Martin could have made a career as a concert pianist if he'd wanted,' she said.

'But instead he lived as a recluse in this house, all because his brother stole his woman,' said Adam with a snort of derision. 'Of course, he could afford to. He sold the family shares in the pulp and paper industry the Jonsons had started in this area over a century ago and invested it, very wisely, in oil stocks so that he could retreat to this house and play his piano to himself.' His voice was harsh and critical. Then he shrugged and said more quietly, 'But who am I to judge him? I'm going the same way, and one day I'll be known, like he was, as that crazy old Jonson man who lives by himself in the house on Pickering Point.'

'Stop it! Stop being so sorry for yourself,' Lenore spoke urgently, almost angrily. 'Oh, you've already got a reputation in the village for being rude. When I told my sister about the way you behaved after we collided on the sidewalk she recognised you immediately.'

'Did she?' The dark eyebrows slanting above the tinted glasses tilted derisively. 'Yet you came walking this way, across my land. Why? To tweak the tail of the wounded lion?' he taunted. 'To find out if he would savage you again?'

'I didn't expect to see you,' she replied coolly. 'This chowder is very good,' she went on, deliberately changing the subject. 'Who is Bertha Smith?'

'A woman from the village who comes three days a week to clean and cook. She and her husband Albert used to work for Martin as caretaker and housekeeper, and when I arrived here they came and offered to do the same for me. They'll be here in the morning—God knows what they'll think when they find you here.' He grinned unkindly. 'It'll be all over the village that I've got a new girl-friend,' he added, standing up and picking up the tray. 'Could you eat some chocolate cake and drink a cup of coffee now?'

'Yes, I could. But let me get them,' she offered.

'No. You wouldn't know where to find anything,' he said coldly. He slanted a glance at her, his lips curving in a sardonic grin. 'And I'm sure you'll be the first to agree that it's good for me to do something for someone else. Takes my mind off brooding about my infirmity.'

He left the room, and Lenore stared at the fire. *They'll think I've got a new girl-friend.* Knowing how the local people liked to gossip about strangers in their midst, she wasn't surprised at the interpretation the Smiths might put on her presence here in the morning.

A *new* girl-friend. Had Adam been making an indirect reference to the woman Blythe had talked about and who had lived here before Christmas? Possibly.

Adam returned to the room, the dog at his heels, and put the tray on the table again. This time there were two plates, each containing a thick wedge of chocolate cake oozing fresh cream and two mugs of coffee together with a small jug of cream and a bowl of sugar. Adam sat down in his chair. Picking up a fork, Lenore sank it into the smooth sponge of the cake, cutting off a morsel and lifting it to her mouth. It melted almost immediately against her palate.

'Have you ever thought of learning Braille?' she asked.

'No. I've told you, I thought I'd be able to see by now,' he replied curtly, and there was another silence, broken only by the crackle of the fire and the faint whisper of music from the radio. The sound of the music suggested another idea to Lenore.

'Do you like music?' she ventured, glancing across at him. With his fair colouring and hefty physique he was a bit leonine, she thought. A caged and wounded lion, tense and wary, growling and snapping when anyone got too close to him, yet sometimes reaching out to touch . . . if one wasn't careful and got too close to him.

'Some.' He was still abrupt, uninterested, as he ate his cake slowly, holding the plate high up so that there wasn't so much chance of him dropping crumbs.

'What sort?'

'My taste is pretty eclectic—modern jazz, some hard rock, a few favourite classical pieces. I like music written for the guitar in particular.' He jerked his head towards the radio. 'This is a tape of Segovia, the famous Spanish guitarist.'

'Yes, I'd noticed,' she told him. 'Have you ever played an instrument?'

'I used to play the guitar. Like most other guys in my age group I used to fancy myself as a rock-and-roller for a time—had hopes of emulating the Beatles or the Rolling Stones.'

'Oh. You played the electric guitar,' she commented.

'And the classical guitar.'

'So you can read music?'

'No. I used to play by ear.'

'Could you play the guitar now?' she asked.

'I don't know. I haven't got a guitar to play. I sold the two I used to own years ago when I was short of cash and wanted to go to college to study cinematography.' He put down his empty plate and felt for his coffee mug. Lenore watched his long fingers feeling for the cream and the sugar, finding both. 'Why all the questions?' he asked, sitting back again, coffee mug in one hand. 'What are you trying to do?'

'Find something for you to do that might help you forget the limitations of your blindness,' she said hesitantly, noticing that his mouth had that savage twist to it again.

'Ha! Fancy yourself as an occupational therapist, do you?' he jeered. 'Well, I don't want your help or your interest.'

'But you can't give up living a full and creative life just because you can't always see,' she protested.

'Can't I? Just you stay around and watch me!'

'Isn't there anyone . . .' she paused, wondering how best to phrase what she wanted to say diplomatically, without offending him, and finding no other way than to ask a direct question she plunged on recklessly. 'Isn't there anyone you could marry? Couldn't you get married, have children, even though you're half blind. Then you'd have some reason for living.'

The dark lenses turned in her direction again as he stared at her for a few silent seconds. Then he said softly,

'Would you marry me?'

The softly spoken words seem to hang in the air insinuatingly and for a moment Lenore was spellbound again, seemingly trapped in the aura of this man, feeling as if she was being drawn inexorably towards him even though she wasn't moving. Her heart raced, she found herself panting for breath, her head felt as if it would burst. Her lips parted as the words, *Yes, I would marry you*, formed in her mind. Almost she said them, them a log fell from the grate in the fireplace, sending up orange sparks behind the fireguard, and the dog yelped in protest, sitting up suddenly. The spell broke. Catching her breath, Lenore bit back what she had been going to say and said instead, quickly and defensively,

'That isn't a fair question!'

'Why isn't it?' he retorted, not at all distracted by the falling log or the disturbed dog, still looking at her through the dark lenses.

'I've only just met you, so I can't answer it,' she stammered, her cheeks flaming.

'Hell, don't get me wrong,' said Adam, his lips thinning in exasperation. 'I wasn't proposing to you. What I meant was would you marry me, half blind as I am, with no future prospects Would any woman in her right mind today want to be tied in marriage to a semi-invalid?'

'It . . . it would depend on how the woman feels about you,' she replied, leaning back in relief; a feeling that was swamped suddenly and unexpectedly by disappointment because his question had not been a proposal after all, causing her to sit up again and mentally shake herself. What was the matter with her? Why was she behaving so irrationally? 'You see, I'd have to be in love with a man before I could consider marrying him,' she went on in a rush. 'And I'd have to be sure he was in love with me. Then it wouldn't matter if he was blind, deaf, lame or even terminally ill, I'd marry him,' she added, her voice growing firm as she stated her long-held philosophy of love.

'In love?' he remarked, jeering again. 'What the hell does that mean? Have you ever been in love with a guy? Are you in love now?'

'Yes, I have been in love, and . . . and . . . I'm in love now.' Her voice faltered on the last few words, because suddenly she was unsure of her feelings for Herzel.

'Going to marry him, then?' Adam seemed to be unkindly amused, his crooked grin carving creases beside his lip corners, and Lenore wished she could have found some way of evading the direct question. 'Well?' he persisted when she didn't answer. 'Are you going to marry the man you're in love with?'

'No.' It came out in a whisper.

'Why not?'

She realised he had manoeuvred her very skilfully into telling him more about herself than she had ever intended to tell him.

'It's none of your business,' she retorted.

'Okay, so I have to guess again, and going by what you've just said about having to be sure the guy was in love with you before marrying him I guess he doesn't return your love. Right?'

'I don't want to talk about it,' Lenore flared.

'But you'd like to be married?' he came back at her, each word rapier-sharp, stabbing at her just as if they were fighting a duel and provoking her to strike back wildly.

'Yes, I would,' she retorted. 'But not just for the sake of being able to say I'm married. I wouldn't and I couldn't marry anyone just to solve any problems I have.'

'So there's the answer to the question you put to me. I wouldn't and couldn't marry *anyone* either, just for the sake of being married or just to solve my present problem of not being able to see properly and not being able to pursue my career,' he replied coldly. 'On the other hand——' he went on, his voice drawling as he stood up and came carefully around the end of the coffee table to sit on the sofa beside her stretched out legs, 'On the other hand,' he repeated, his lips curving in a faint enigmatic smile as he leaned towards her, 'I wouldn't mind having a woman to live with me right now. A woman to share my bed at night; a woman not too innocent—I'm not interested in coy virgins who don't know how to make love—a woman who could meet me halfway and match passion with passion, who has come to terms with her own sexuality.' He paused dramatically and leaned even closer to her, resting one hand on the back of the sofa as he hovered over her like a predatory golden eagle about to swoop down and devastate its pray. 'A woman like you, Lenore,' he murmured, his voice deep and suggestive.

Once again she was trapped by his aura, that subtle emanation of his strong yet unpredictable personality that floated about her mysteriously, holding her captive.

'No,' she whispered weakly, trying desperately to destroy the spell. 'No, I couldn't. I couldn't live with you, share your bed.'

'But you want to,' he insisted. 'We could start tonight. We could do it now.' He raised a big hand and his fingers trailed delicately over her cheek, down to her throat, under her hair to the nape of her neck, and immediately tiny shivers of delight rippled through her. Her body began to play traitor to her will.

'You ... you're crazy,' she stuttered, 'out of your mind, if you ... you think that I can go to bed and make love with you right now and then ... and then live with you in this house!'

'Perhaps I am crazy. Wild with wanting some comfort and satisfaction,' he conceded. 'But then so are you, Lenore, so are you, so why don't we join forces and give each other what we both crave?'

'But you said you wished I hadn't come this

way,' she argued, stalling for time, afraid of the temptation offered by his lips and the caress of his long fingers. 'You said I wasn't welcome here.'

'I know I did.' His crooked grin appeared and her heart flip-flopped. 'I was railing against fate for having sent someone like you into my life at this particular moment.' He paused and, fascinated, she watched his tongue lick his lower lip. 'Ever since I found you outside in the snow this afternoon I've been trying to protect you against me,' he whispered, 'but I can't any more, Lenore. I want you, and I'm going to have you.'

'No!' She shrieked the word at him, and as his mouth swooped to hers she slid from under him, rolling off the sofa to the floor, landing there on all fours and crawling away until she was in an open space and could stand up. Then in a lurching run she made for the doorway, not sure where she was going or even why she was going, obeying a primitive instinct to protect her femaleness against a male predator, afraid of being raped and yet acknowledging reluctantly that if Adam caught her and made love to her it wouldn't be rape. It would be the coming together of two lost persons in need of comfort and love.

Out into the hall she limped and across through another doorway into a dark room. Behind the open door she slid and leaned against the wall, her heart fluttering in her breast, her ears straining to catch the sound of Adam's footsteps.

In the silence of the dark room she could hear the flutter of snowflakes against glass window panes and the whine of the wind. In the shaft of dim light that slanted into the room from the hallway she could see the pattern on the carpet, the gleam of furniture. Then suddenly the door was swung away from her. It crashed closed and no light shafted into the room any more. Only faint snowlight glimmered at two long windows.

'Clever of you, Lenore!' Adam's voice held a note of mockery and the sound of it made her tense against the wall. She had not realised he had come into the room before shutting the door. 'Clever of you to come into this room, because this is where I intended to bring you later tonight to share my bed.'

He was, she realised with a strange shiver of excitement, quite close to her again, although she couldn't make out exactly where he was standing.

'Adam,' she said, trying to sound calm, hoping to reason with him, 'please don't do it. Don't do anything you . . . you might regret later.'

He didn't reply, but she heard him move towards her and wished she hadn't spoken. By speaking she had betrayed her position to him; before, he hadn't known where she was. Teeth biting hard into her lower lip, she slid along the wall away from the door and, she hoped, from him, holding her breath so that he wouldn't hear it. Then when she thought she was clear of him she lunged forward, moving as fast as her damaged knee would allow her, hoping to go around him and find the door, open it and escape into the hallway again.

She was on her way when he reached out a long arm and caught her around the waist, hauling her against him roughly so that for a few moments she lay limp and breathless. With his free hand he groped and found her face. His hard fingers gripped her chin, forcing it up. Around her waist his arm was an iron band crushing her against him. There wasn't any way she could avoid the assault of his mouth on hers.

For several moments Lenore hung helplessly in that tight embrace while Adam's hard hot lips ravaged hers. His mouth took possession passionately, and something seemed to explode in her mind. No longer did he need to hold her against him, because she pressed herself invitingly against him, twisting a little, inciting his further arousal with subtle movements of her breasts and hips.

Hands at her waist, he pushed her lightly away from him.

'Now tell me you don't want to do it,' he scoffed breathlessly. 'Now tell me you don't want me to carry you to my bed in this room and make love to you, that you don't want me to smooth your clothes away from your body and to touch you until you're on fire with desire. Now tell me that—and you'll commit perjury.' Suddenly, as if becoming impatient with his own rhetoric, he jerked her towards him again, 'Lenore, I want you now. I want to make love to you. Do you still want to stop me?'

'But not in the dark,' she whispered. 'Oh, not in the dark. I . . . I want to be able to see your eyes, the colour of them. I don't know the colour of your eyes. Please, Adam, put on some lights.'

That she had surprised him by her request she could tell, because his hands went lax at her waist and he laughed a little.

'So be it. I'll put on some light and you shall see the colour of my eyes if it will make you happy,' he agreed.

As she had hoped, he let go of her completely and she heard him move away from her. Immediately she sidestepped in the direction of the door, her hands outstretched behind her as she backed towards it until they touched the wooden panels. Turning, she groped for and found the doorknob and twisted it. She pulled the door open and rushed limpingly into the hallway just as Adam switched on the bedside lamp in the room behind her.

No point in going out through the front door into the raging blizzard of the spring storm, thought Lenore. To her left an elegant staircase swept upwards into the mysterious darkness of the second floor. Hearing Adam roar her name, hearing the soft pad of his feet coming across the floor of the room behind her, she limped wincingly towards the staircase and up.

'Lenore—where are you? Where the hell have you gone?' shouted Adam, and she spared a glance over her shoulder at him. Hands on his hips, he stood in the hallway, his head tipped to one side as if he was listening intently for the sound of movements, so she stopped going up the stairs and held her breath, her heart thumping so loudly she was sure he would be able to hear it.

Then he moved towards the living room, and letting out her breath she crept up the rest of the stairs, letting the velvety darkness swallow her.

She didn't go much further because she was afraid of walking into something unseen, and also she wanted to see down into the hallway so that she would know where Adam would go next. Leaning on the wooden railing that edged the upper landing, she recovered her breath and listened to her heartbeats slow down, and for the first time found a certain amount of humour in the situation. It was like a game she had once played as a child at parties when one child had been blindfolded with a scarf tied over his eyes and had been turned around three times to disorientate him. Then he had had to try and catch as many of the other children as he could while they had danced and dodged about him tormentingly.

A sound from below drew her attention. Caesar was coming out of the living room, closely followed by Adam. The dog stopped at the bottom of the stairs, sniffing, then looked up the stairs and growled softly. Adam said something to the dog and it began to slink up the stairs. He groped with one hand for the banister, found it and began to walk up the stairs too.

'Oh no!' Lenore gasped and, turning, fled along the pitch dark landing, trailing one hand along the wall as she went, hoping to find a doorway leading into a room where she could hide. Her fingers had just hit a wooden frame when she heard another sound from the stairway; the sound of someone tripping and then falling down the stairs, bumping against each tread.

'Oh no!' she gasped again, realising that Adam had missed a stair and had fallen. She blundered back to the head of the stairs, in time to see Caesar loping down them. On the floor of the hallway at the foot of the stairs Adam lay supine on the floor. *Motionless.*

'Oh no!' Lenore gasped again, and sped down the stairs, forgetful of the pain in her knee. The dog, which was now sitting guard over Adam's body, growled at her again. Ignoring that warning, frantic now because what had been a humorous situation showed signs of becoming a disaster, she flung herself on her knees beside Adam, wincing sharply when her right knee hit the hard floor.

'Oh, what happened? What happened?' she cried helplessly, staring down at him, wanting to touch him somewhere but afraid to. He didn't move.

Was he dead? How could she tell if he was or not? Oh, how useless she was when it came to anything like this! She knew nothing about first aid. She leaned over him, searching his face intently. The dark glasses were still in place; they hadn't been knocked off when he had fallen. She would take them off to see if his eyes were open or closed.

Her hands were just reaching out to the glasses to lift them away from his eyes when he moved swiftly, one arm swinging up and around her shoulders, pulling her down on top of him and holding her there.

'Got you!' he whispered in her ear, which was against his lips.

She didn't try to wriggle free. She was too relieved to know that he wasn't badly hurt. Turning her head, she expressed that relief by kissing him frankly on the lips.

He groaned softly deep in his throat. Immediately she lifted her mouth from his and tried to sit up, but couldn't, because he was still holding her down against him.

'Adam, what is it? Are you ... are you badly hurt?' she whispered, touching his cheek with gentle fingers.

'Uhuh.' He groaned again and twisted his head from side to side. 'My head—I banged the back of it when I fell,' he told her.

'Why did you fall? What happened?' she asked, trying to get away from him again. He was stroking her back now, slowly, caressingly, suggestively, right from her shoulder to her buttocks, and her whole body seemed to be melting, flowing against his.

'I tripped,' he replied. 'One of the reasons I have my bedroom on the ground floor is so that I don't have to go upstairs. I have trouble in judging the height of the stair treads.'

'Then why did you come up the stairs just now?'

'I wanted you,' he whispered. 'I still want you. Let's go to bed.'

His hand swept up to the back of her head. His fingers tangled in her hair and he forced her face down to his. Slowly and sensually his tongue traced the shape of her lips, and something inside her seemed to burst into flame. Heat scorched through her body. Her thighs burned and tensed, and her breasts swelled.

The arrogant intimacy of his caressing tongue wasn't enough. She wanted more. She wanted his lips. Hands framing his face, she pressed her mouth against his. With another groan Adam put both arms around her as he lay back on the floor, holding her closely on top of him, pressing all of her against all of him until she could feel the urgent desperation of his need pulsing through him, inciting an even greater arousal of her own desire.

'Not here,' he whispered at last against her lips, and she came down from the heaven of ecstasy to the reality of the hard oak floor. Still holding her, he sat up, and somehow without letting go of each other they both stood up. For a moment they stood face to face, Adam's hands at her waist, her hands resting on his arms. It was a moment of hesitancy, as if they both felt they were standing on the edge of a precipice of commitment and were undecided about whether to plunge in or withdraw.

'Coming to bed with me?' asked Adam softly.

'What if I say no?' she challenged.

'I'll probably shoot myself,' he said, his lips twisting bitterly.

She was horrified by his reply. Her hands tightening on his arms, she tried to shake him rebukingly.

'Adam, you mustn't say that. It isn't funny,' she whispered.

'I wasn't being funny,' he said darkly. 'I've been considering my options ever since that surgeon told me the truth about my sight. Shooting myself is one of them.'

'No, oh no!' Her hands slid up to his neck and her arms wound around it. 'No, you musn't take your own life. You mustn't! I . . . I couldn't bear it if you did.'

'Then you'll come to bed with me now, make love with me?' he whispered, his arms binding her to him again.

'Yes, I'll come to bed with you now,' she replied steadily, giving in to her own desire as much as to his.

He swept her off her feet then and carried her surely and strongly into the bedroom, where lamplight slanted across a wide bed. Setting her down on her feet beside the bed, he went back to close the door and stepped back to stand before her, bending his head slightly towards her.

'You can take my glasses off if you want,' he said, his hands going to her waist again as if he had to hold her, touch her somewhere in case she ran away from him again.

Gently she removed the glasses. Wide-set eyes, slate blue in colour, seemed to look back at her. *Seemed to*, only. For they did not focus. There was no life in those blurred irises. The black pupils did not contract to adjust to the soft lighting of the room, and thinking of how once they must have looked bright with mockery, sharp with anger, sparkling with intelligence, Lenore felt riven with empathy, her whole heart reaching out to him.

'Well?' he asked, his voice harsh. 'How do they look?'

'They look . . .' she began, and put the glasses down carefully on the bedside table. 'They look,' she went on, turning back to him and framing his face with her hands again, 'like the eyes of a man I could love.'

And drawing his face down she kissed each eye. His response was instantaneous. With a muttered oath he lifted her again and laid her down on the bed. Lying beside her, holding her tightly, he covered her face and her throat with hot savage kisses while his hands began to search her body, reaching under her sweater to curve about her breasts, and from then on there was no sanity, only the sweet torment, the wild frenzy of physical desire.

Clothes were removed and were tossed aside, and for a moment of calm in the eye of the passionate storm they touched and fondled each other admiringly, worshipping silken skin and smooth curves, tantalising delicate nerve endings until passion began to beat along their veins again and in an agony of desire they fused together and seemed to soar like a rocket beyond pain, beyond reason into the blue emptiness of infinite space where they burst in an explosion of ecstatic sensation.

'Lenore . . .' Through the spinning aftermath of sensual pleasure she heard Adam speak to her, his voice slightly slurred as if he were intoxicated; satiated with pleasure. 'Are you all right?'

'Yes. It was good. For you too?' she murmured drowsily.

'It was good. Thank you.' She felt him lift her hand and brush the back of it with warm lips as if in homage, and then she was whirling down and down into the dark oblivion of sleep.

CHAPTER FOUR

A BEAM of early morning sunlight, slanting in through the east facing window of the room downstairs that had been turned into a bedroom for Adam Jonson, danced on Lenore's closed eyelids, teasing them to open. For a moment, eyelashes drooping, she considered closing her eyes again and slipping back into the deep slumber that she had been enjoying. After all, there was no urgency to get up this morning. No one was staying at the Inn, so she didn't have to help Blythe with the breakfast. She could sleep in, if she wanted.

Closing her eyes, she stretched her legs. Something seemed to sting her right knee as if a pinpoint had been jabbed into it and her foot touched something hard and warm; something smooth yet hairy; another leg.

Wide awake now, shocked into wakefulness and awareness by these unusual sensations, she sat up quickly, sheet and blanket falling away from her, revealing her nakedness, the upward sweep of pink-tipped breasts, the smooth creamy curve of shoulders. Memory of what had happened during the night washed over her and she groaned softly and covered her face with her hands.

What had she done? Oh, what had she done? And all of her own free will too.

Slowly she lowered her hands and glanced

sideways. Beside her, his back to her, Adam slept. Sunlight burnished his bare shoulders and glinted on his tousled pale hair. Remembering how much she had exulted in his strength and masculine beauty when he had been making love to her, Lenore smiled a small mysterious smile of satisfaction. It was good to know she had been wanted and had been possessed by such a man; to know that for a short time she had been able to release him from the torment in which he had been living.

Her hand was reaching out to touch him, to stroke the smooth broad back, when she heard the dog barking somewhere at the back of the house. Withdrawing her hand, she listened. Were those voices she could hear? Outside or inside?

She remembered suddenly that Adam had said the Smiths would be coming this morning. They must have come, and any minute now one of them would be coming to this room looking for Adam. She must not be found here in bed with him.

Quickly she rolled out of bed and began to collect up her scattered clothing. As she pulled on her jeans she spared the time to look at her right knee. It was badly bruised but not as swollen as she had expected. When she touched the swollen place a sharp pinprick went through it, making her wince.

When she was dressed she gave the sleeping Adam another glance, wondering whether to wake him or not, decided against waking him since he was sleeping so peacefully and limped to the door. Turning the knob as quietly as she could, she opened the door, slid through the narrow space into the hallway and closed the door after her. She stood for a moment listening again and heard quite distinctly the voice of a woman speaking in a room somewhere at the end of a passage which led off the hallway to the back of the house.

Moving as quietly as she could, she went into the living room. Sunlight showed up the dust on wooden surfaces. The rosewood piano glowed with ruby-coloured highlights. The fire was out, the hearth full of grey wood-ash. On the marble overmantle the elegant ormolu clock struck the hour. Seven o'clock. She had just pulled on her jacket and was about to pull on her boots when she heard footsteps coming along the hallway. They came straight to the living room and a woman, short and sturdy in stretch-knit brown pants and a brown and beige striped sweater came in. She had grey hair and her round face shone with good health. When she saw Lenore her light hazel eyes widened with surprise and she dropped the Electrolux vacuum cleaner she was carrying to the floor.

'Land sakes!' she exclaimed. 'Who are you, and what are you doing here?'

Having zipped up her boots, Lenore got to her feet and smiled. She knew exactly how she was going to handle this situation.

'You must be Bertha Smith,' she said. 'Adam told me you'd be here this morning to clean up. I'm Lenore Parini—my sister owns the Northport Inn. I got caught in the storm when I was walking this way last night and hurt my knee, so Adam let me stay the night. We couldn't let anyone know I was here because his phone was out of order. I'm so glad you've come. Are the roads very bad?'

'Seen worse,' said Bertha Smith with typical down-east brevity, her yellowish eyes, narrowed now in suspicion, flicking over Lenore's clothing. 'Hurt your knee, eh? How?'

'I banged it when I fell. It swelled up and I couldn't walk properly. Do you think your husband would drive me to the Inn now? I'd like to get back—my sister must be out of her mind with worry!'

'I dunno if he will or he won't. You'd best ask him yourself,' replied Bertha surlily. 'He's in the kitchen feeding the dog.' Her glance fell on the tray on the coffee table, studied the two coffee mugs and two plates.

'Thank you,' said Lenore, picking up her hat and mitts and beginning to limp towards the doorway. There she paused and looked back. 'Your chowder was very good, by the way,' she said. 'So was the chocolate cake.'

But all Bertha Smith did was snort and mutter something about some women being mighty loose in their behaviour, staying overnight with men they weren't married to, so Lenore hurried away down the passage to the kitchen to find Albert Smith, hoping he would be more friendly than his wife was.

He was a tall thin man dressed in thick denim overalls and checked woollen shirt. He had a long blue-chinned cadaverous face and didn't seem at all surprised to see her. He listened to her explanation, all the time watching her with bright blue eyes, his jaws moving rhythmically as he chewed gum.

'About time Adam got himself another woman,' he remarked sardonically when she had finished. 'It ain't healthy for a man like him to live without a woman. You sure now you want to go back to the Inn?'

'Of course I'm sure. I have to let my sister know I'm still alive and I have to go to the hospital to have my knee looked at. I really did hurt it, you know, and I'll be glad if you'll drive me.'

'Told Adam you're leaving?' he asked.

'No—he's still asleep. But he knows I want to go. It was his idea that you should drive me back.'

He considered her thoughtfully, still chewing his gum.

'Don't rightly hold with you leaving before he wakes up,' he muttered. 'Reckon I'll go and tell him.' He took a stride towards the doorway leading into the passage. 'Don't want him cussing me for driving you back to Northport without letting him know.'

'But it will be all right, really it will,' argued Lenore, going after him and sliding between him and the door. 'Please, Mr Smith, let's go now. I want to get back before my sister tells the police I'm missing. And Adam won't cuss you—he doesn't want me to stay any longer. He'll be glad I've gone when you tell him, I know he will.'

Again Albert frowned as he stared down at her.

'You known Adam long?' he asked.

'No. Only since yesterday when I asked him if I could use his phone. He didn't want to help me. He didn't want me to stay, so he won't be angry if I leave.'

'Okay, then,' sighed Albert. 'Guess it's none of my business.' Turning on his heel, he went over to the back door where his parka hung on a hook. He pulled on the jacket, covered his head with a visored cap and opened the back door. 'Truck's right outside, ma'am,' he said politely. 'Watch your step now on them steps—they're some slippery.'

The truck was a blue Ford pick-up. Lenore had a little difficulty in getting up into the cab because of the pain in her knee, but with a boost from behind from Albert she made it into the passenger's seat, and soon, guided by Albert, the truck was trundling down the driveway from which the snow had been ploughed to the sides by the snow-plough on the front of the truck when Albert and Bertha had driven to the house that morning.

The sky was blue and sun-flushed, arching above smooth white curves of snow. Against the blue the dark green feathery branches of pines and the pinkish blur of elm and birch branches were delicately etched. A flock of dark birds, disturbed by the noise of the truck, rose from the trees edging the boundary of the Jonson land. Compared with the stormy night the morning was serene and bright, and Lenore felt in tune with it. She too felt calm and hopeful now that the dark surging passion that had sprung between her and Adam Jonson had been culminated. She could only hope that he felt the same.

Out through the stone gateposts the truck trundled and turned right following the curve of Pickering Lane under the slanting shadows of the trees. As the lane changed direction, arrowing straight towards Main Street, houses appeared on either side, white clapboard gleaming against white snow in the yellow sunlight.

'Reckon the snow will soon be gone if the sun keeps shining like this,' drawled the laconic Albert. 'Temperature's up already.' He slanted her a glance from under the visor of his cap. 'You stayin' long at the Inn?'

'I'm not sure,' replied Lenore. She could also be laconic when she wished; as laconic as any Mainer.

'Adam and me are cousins,' was the next surprising remark.

'Really? How come?'

'My mother was a maid at the house way back when Albert Jonson—he was the father of Adam's father—was alive. She had a daughter, who was also Albert's daughter, born wrong side of blanket, as they used to say in the old days. Albertine, she was called. She was my mother and half-sister to Martin and Adam Jonson. That makes me cousin to this Adam's father and second cousin to Adam himself. Time was I kind of believed I'd inherit the property, being the only direct descendant of Albert Jonson. Or so it seemed.'

'You must have been disappointed, then, when you found out Martin had left everything to his brother's grandson,' said Lenore gently.

'Reckon I was, until I met Adam.' He gave her another sidelong glance. 'I went to visit him when he was in that hospital just to make sure he was the right Jonson. Soon as I see him I knew we were kin. Even though he was blind and his face was all cut up he was the spittin' image of

my grandfather and Adam's great-grandfather,
Albert Jonson. He's like him in other ways too—
likes women and attracts them the same way
honey attracts bees. Know what I mean?'

'Yes, I think so,' muttered Lenore, thinking
ruefully of the way she had been attracted to
Adam last night, drawn to him against her will.

'When I saw what a bad way he was in,' Albert
went on, 'I didn't feel disappointed any more
about not getting the property. I guess I realised
he needed the place more than I did. He needed
somewhere to go to, a home to hide in while he
recovered. So I arranged for him to come here
and Bertha and I have looked after him ever
since, just like we looked after Martin Jonson.'

'That was kind of you,' she said.

'Least I could do for me own flesh and blood,'
retorted Albert fiercely. 'Don't hold with folks
who can't help their own kin.'

'But I thought there was someone else living
with him when he first came. My sister told me
there was a woman staying with him,' probed
Lenore curiously.

'That bitch!' Albert's voice was harsh with
scorn and Lenore had the impression he would
have liked to spit. 'She turned up after he'd
moved into the house—seems she'd been his girl-
friend once. Anyway, she moved in too for a
while. Don't rightly know what happened, but
they had a dust-up one day and she left. Reckon
Adam didn't like her living here.'

'He doesn't seem too happy about what the
surgeon told him about his eyesight,' Lenore
remarked.

'Told you about that, did he?' queried Albert

on a note of surprise. 'He must have taken to you, then. Adam doesn't talk about his problems to everyone.'

The brakes squealed and the truck came to a sliding, skidding stop at the junction with Main Street. Albert turned it into the wide tree-lined street and in a few seconds was braking it to a stop again in front of the heaps of snow in front of the Inn.

'Thanks for the lift,' said Lenore.

'You're welcome. Take care now,' replied Albert.

She got out of the truck, gave him a parting wave and limped up the narrow pathway that someone had cleared to the front door. The door was unlocked and as she stepped into the panelled hallway the warmth of the Inn seemed to close around her, enfolding her and making her feel welcome.

'Blythe. Blythe, I'm back!' she called.

'Thank God!' Blythe came hurrying into the lounge from the kitchen. She was still in her dressing gown, a fluffy blue thing, and her black hair was loose on her shoulders. Dark circles were scored under her wide anxious eyes. 'Thank God you're alive!' she added, putting her arms around Lenore and hugging her. 'Where have you been? What happened? I've been sick with worry all night—haven't slept a wink! Josh and I set out to look for you, but the storm was too bad. We got stuck in his car on the road to the lighthouse and had to walk back here. Oh, I don't know what I'd have done if he hadn't stayed with me!'

'I'm sorry,' said Lenore. 'I knew you'd be anxious. But I couldn't do anything about it. You see, I hurt my knee and couldn't walk very well and Adam Jonson's phone was out of order, so I couldn't contact you.'

'Adam Jonson? You've been in the Jonson house?' exclaimed Blythe.

'Yes. I was near there when I fell and hurt my knee. It was the only place I could get to. If he'd had a car I'd have tried to get back here, but he doesn't have one because he can't see to drive.'

'Then how did you get here now?'

'Albert Smith drove me. He works for Adam. So does his wife.'

'Oh, lord!' groaned Blythe. 'Now it will be all over the village that you stayed the night with Adam Jonson ... alone, and everyone will think the worst.'

'Well, I can't help that,' Lenore snapped. 'I didn't ask to be stranded in his house.'

'I know you didn't,' said Blythe soothingly. 'Come into the kitchen and have some breakfast and tell me what's wrong with your knee.' She gave Lenore another quick hug, 'Oh, you've no idea how relieved I am to see you! It must have been an ordeal for you as well as for me. I hope Adam Jonson behaved himself and treated you well.'

'He was a bit feisty at first, wouldn't let me into his house to use his phone, but when he realised I'd really hurt myself he was more amicable,' replied Lenore coolly as she limped after Blythe and through to the kitchen.

The man with greying dark hair and a lean weatherbeaten face, who was sitting at the table rose to his feet as she and Blythe entered the kitchen.

'Lenore, I'd like you to meet Josh Kyd,' said Blythe a little shyly.

'Glad to see you're all in one piece,' said Josh as he shook hands with Lenore. 'We were just thinking of informing the police that you were missing.' His sleepy grey eyes warmed with affection as he looked past her at Blythe. 'Guess I can leave you now and go to the boatyard. Time I was starting work.'

'Yes, yes, of course.' Blythe was actually blushing rosily, Lenore noted as she sat down at the table and stretched her right leg before her.

'I'll come round this evening,' Josh added as he moved towards the back door, 'and we can talk some more about those plans.'

'Thanks, Josh, thanks for staying,' said Blythe, following.

'Any time,' he replied, turning to give Blythe what Lenore could only describe as a meaningful look. 'See you.'

He went out, and Blythe slowly closed the door. Smiling a little to herself, she went across to the cooking range, lit a burner and put some butter into a heavy cast-iron frying pan.

'Could you eat an omelette?' she asked Lenore.

'I could eat a house,' replied Lenore. 'Any coffee?'

'Sure.' Blythe came across to the table with the coffee pot and a mug, poured and set the mug before her sister, then wandered back to the cooking range.

'He's nice,' said Lenore as she poured cream into the hot coffee.

'Who is?' queried Blythe, pouring beaten eggs into the smoking melted butter. 'Adam Jonson?'

'No, you fool—Josh Kyd. Are you in love with him?'

'I don't know,' said Blythe slowly. 'I think I might be, but we're really just friends.'

'That's how the best romances are supposed to start—with friendship,' mused Lenore.

'My, listen to you!' mocked Blythe. 'Are you speaking from experience? Or have you been reading Ann Landers' column lately? Tell me about your knee.'

Taking the hint that Blythe didn't want to discuss her friendship with Josh Kyd any more, Lenore explained what had happened to her knee, and it was decided that she should go to the hospital outpatient department as soon as she had finished breakfast and had changed her clothes.

Blythe drove her to the hospital, where she was seen by the doctor on duty, who recommended an X-ray on the knee as he thought she might have cracked the knee-cap. The X-ray showed a fine hairline crack that he said would heal fairly quickly as long as she didn't walk on her right leg too much.

'I could put a cast on it to make you keep it stiff,' he said. 'But if you're prepared to obey my instructions that won't be necessary. Rest it as much as you can and if you have to walk about use a pair of crutches. Come back in a week and I'll have another look at it.'

Pleased that her injury wasn't too serious, Lenore went with Blythe to the local pharmacy, where they were able to rent a pair of crutches, then they returned to the Inn.

The next few days passed by slowly and uneventfully. At first Lenore was glad to lie

about the lounge with her right leg propped up.
To keep herself entertained she caught up on
her reading, and she also practised playing her
clarinet, and she had Blythe for company when
her sister wasn't busy preparing lunches and
serving them or cooking dinners for the few local
people who came during the week to dine at the
Inn.

But as time went by she became less and less
interested in reading and found herself day-
dreaming instead, and as if it wasn't enough that
the hours she spent alone at night in bed were
filled with thoughts and memories of Adam
Jonson, he began to invade and take over her
daydreams too.

How was he? What was he doing? Would she
ever see him again? Did he think of her and
wonder if he would see her again?

Or had their brief and passionate encounter
been an only once in a lifetime happening? A
white-hot, sensual coming together of two lonely
and rejected people? A flash-fire blazing up
brilliantly for a short while before dying out just
as swiftly as it had flared up?

Ten to one Adam Jonson, having satisfied his
overwhelming physical need to make love to a
woman, had forgotten by now that she had stayed
with him for a night, she thought with a touch of
cynicism. Men were like that—they soon forgot.
And she must learn to forget too.

Forget the magical touch of Adam's fingertips
stroking her skin? Forget the heat of his lips on
hers? Forget the hard pressure of his thighs
against hers? Forget, forget. Oh, how could she
forget?

He had made love to her the way she had often secretly dreamed of being made love to. He had made love to her as Herzel never had. Savage and tender in turn, he had aroused in her sensations she hadn't known she was capable of feeling. He had created a new Lenore, a woman with no past and no future, a wholly sensual person aflame with desire.

Oh, she must forget. She must forget, or she would be running to him as soon as her knee was better. She would be trampling her pride in the dust and pleading with him to take her and do with her what he wished. She would be kneeling before him like a slave before a master, submitting, and that was something she had vowed long ago she would never do to any man.

'Lenore?' Blythe called from the kitchen where she was preparing dinner. 'Phone for you. Take it on the extension in there.'

'For me?' Her hands were suddenly clammy and shaking. Her heart skipped a beat and began to race. Her cheeks burned. Could Adam be calling her at last? To ask why she had left his house before he had wakened?'

'Who is it?' she called back.

'Isaac Goldstein.'

Disappointment was a cold wave washing over her. She reached for the phone, picked up the receiver and spoke. Isaac answered her. He was calling, he said, to remind her that the music group would be meeting at his house that evening and he would be pleased if she came. Lenore promised to be there. He thanked her and hung up.

Blythe drove her to the Goldstein house. It was an old Cape Cod cottage on Bay Street East, with views of the estuary and the green hills of the other shore. In the living-room, that was crammed with antique furniture, Lenore shared a velvet-covered love-seat with another new member of the group, a young man called Douglas Corwen, who played the cello.

'Tonight I'd like to discuss our future,' said Isaac. 'I'm hoping that our new members will be able to offer some ideas and alternatives. I'm pleased to tell you that we have found a cellist at last and so our string quartet is complete. We should be ready to put on a concert at the beginning of next month, that is on June the first. That gives us just a month to rehearse, this being the second of May. It also gives us some time to find a location for the concert. I've approached the three churches in the village, but while each church organisation is willing to let us rent either the church halls or the church buildings, I don't find any of them suitable.'

There followed a lot of discussion. Members asked Isaac what sort of place he envisaged as being the perfect setting for the concert, and as she listened Lenore found herself remembering the long wide room at the Jonson house, the rosewood piano, the velvet curtains, the long windows opening in summer on to a terrace with a view of Penobscot Bay and the Camden Hills. When there was a pause in the discussion she leaned forward and said,

'There's a beautiful Steinway grand in the Jonson house at Pickering Point. There's also a room which must have been designed for the performance of chamber music. All you would need to get would be chairs for the audience.'

'You've seen it?' demanded Isaac, flashing her a bright sharp glance from small brown eyes. 'You've been in the house?'

'Yes, I've been in the house. It would be a great place to hold an annual music festival in,' said Lenore, warming to her theme. 'In fact, with all those rooms and all that land around it it could be developed into a summer cultural centre.'

'Something like Wolf Trap, you mean?' suggested Jack Kenata, leaning forward, his slanting eyes beginning to sparkle with enthusiasm. 'But that's what I've been dreaming about for this area. That's why I got the music group started.'

'Yes,' said Lenore, nodding. 'Something like Wolf Trap,' she repeated. She knew the open-air centre for the performing arts that had been donated to the nation and had, in fact, performed there one summer in a woodwind quartet with Herzel.

'But the property on Pickering Point is a private residence,' remarked Fred Caplan. 'And the guy who owns it and lives in it right now isn't exactly approachable,' he added dryly. 'I can't see Adam Jonson letting any of us in the place. He's very reclusive—even more so than his great-uncle was.' He gave Lenore a curious glance. 'How come you know what it's like inside?'

'I was there last Monday,' replied Lenore coolly, hoping he wouldn't question her more closely.

'Adam Jonson?' queried Janet Moore, another new member of the group. 'He wouldn't be the Adam Jonson who made that documentary film about the fighting in the Middle East, would he? You know, the one who won an award for the best news documentary a few years back?'

'He's that Adam Jonson,' said Fred.

'I'd no idea he lived near Northport,' exclaimed Janet excitedly. 'Do you know him well?' she turned towards Lenore.

'No, not really,' said Lenore.

'Oh, I've just had the greatest idea,' said Willa Caplan. 'If we could get Adam Jonson to agree to let us perform our first concert in his house maybe he would film it for us and it could be shown on TV.'

'He's blind,' said Fred Caplan. 'His days of filming the news or anything else are over. Anyway, we might as well forget the idea. As I've said, he's most unapproachable.'

'There'd be no harm in asking him,' said Jack. He looked at Lenore. 'You know him. Would you be willing to ask him?'

'Would you?' asked Isaac, looking at her earnestly and hopefully. 'From what you've told us the place sounds ideal.'

'I suppose I could go and see him and ask him,' Lenore replied slowly.

'Great!' said Jack enthusiastically.

'But when will you need to know?'

'Before the end of the month, of course,' replied Isaac. 'Meanwhile, we'll continue to look for other suitable premises. And now, before we start rehearsing the quartet, I'd like to discuss the addition to our repertoire of pieces that would include you and Janet. You both have, no doubt, favourite chamber music written for woodwind instruments that you would like to perform, possibly accompanied by piano or even by strings.'

The rest of the evening was spent talking and playing music. Isaac's wife Rose served coffee and cakes and they all left just before midnight, Jack Kanata driving Lenore back to the Inn.

Once she was in bed she lay awake, wondering what she had let herself in for by offering to ask Adam if he would lend the living room of his house for a concert. Where had the idea come from? Had it arisen from a subconscious desire to go and see him again? Probably. And she had seized the excuse quickly, almost greedily.

But she couldn't do it. She couldn't go straight to him and ask him. She would have to phone him first.

For several days she dithered, rehearsing what she would say to him when she got through to him, but each time she picked up the receiver her courage failed her and she didn't dial his number.

She visited the hospital again about her knee, and another X-ray showed that the crack was closing up nicely. The doctor advised her to start putting her weight on it as long as she didn't overdo the walking yet.

Another few days went by. Another weekend came and with it an influx of guests to the Inn. It was Sunday brunch again and Isaac and Jack were there, asking her if she had approached Adam Jonson.

'No, not yet. I ... I haven't been able to get hold of him. I'll try tomorrow,' she said.

But when tomorrow came she was still hesitant, and she confided in Blythe about her offer to go and ask Adam if he would lend his living room for the concert.

'And now you're afraid to go and beard the lion

in his den, I suppose,' mocked Blythe as she parked the car in front of the Inn. 'Why are you afraid of him?' she asked, turning to Lenore as she switched off the car's engine.

'I'm not really afraid of *him*,' replied Lenore thoughtfully. 'I just don't want him to think that I'm making the most of our very brief association by asking him if the music group can hold their concert in his living room. Oh, I wish now that I'd never made the suggestion. Why do I do it, Blythe? Why am I always getting into awkward predicaments? Why can't I learn to keep my mouth shut?'

'I guess it's because you're impulsive and generous, always thinking you can help someone.' Blythe gave her sister a curious sidelong glance. 'Maybe, subconsciously, you want to help Adam Jonson, blast him out of his seclusion by making him show an interest in the community he's come to live in. You always did have a tendency to want to help lame dogs.'

'Yes, I did, didn't I?' agreed Lenore with a sigh. 'And it would be good for him. It would give him something to think about instead of brooding about his infirmity. I'll go and phone him now.'

'That's my sister!' mocked Blythe. 'She's afraid of neither man or beast. And remember, he can't bite you over the phone. He can only roar. And if he does you can always hang up and try again when he's in a softer, more approachable mood.'

Lenore didn't get through to Adam until halfway through the afternoon, and then the phone rang six times before it was answered.

'Hello. Who's calling?' Adam's voice was gruff and abrupt, and she tried hard not to feel put off.

'Adam?' She made an effort to sound cheerful. 'This is Lenore.'

'Who?' he demanded sharply.

Oh lord, he'd forgotten her already! She was tempted to hang up rather than to start explaining who she was; rather than remind him of their night together.

'Lenore Parini.' She forced herself to continue brightly. 'Remember? I got caught in the snowstorm, the weekend before last, and had to stay the night at your house.'

There was silence at the other end of the line. A long silence. And she was just beginning to wonder if Adam was still there or if they had been inadvertently cut off when he spoke again, softly,

'I remember. I remember waking up the next morning and you'd gone.' There was another silence, then he said curtly. 'What do you want? Why have you phoned?'

'I . . . I have a request to make,' she said, and broke off to swallow. For some reason her throat was very dry.

'Request?' he repeated roughly. 'For yourself? What do you want? Money?'

'No, oh, no! Oh, how could you think that!' She was suddenly furious. 'Oh, really, you have the most suspicious mind—and now I wish I hadn't called you . . .'

'So why don't you hang up?' he interrupted her rudely. 'I'm going to.'

There was a clatter at the other end of the line and then a dead silence. Angrily Lenore returned her receiver to its rest and sat glaring for a few minutes at the phone while she called Adam Jonson all the rude names she could think of.

Then, springing to her feet, she went into the kitchen where Blythe was kneading bread dough for dinner rolls.

'He hung up on me!' she spluttered. 'He thought I was going to ask him for money. Oh, he's the most infuriating person I've ever met!'

'What are you going to do now?' asked Blythe in her calm way. 'Give up?'

'No—never!' seethed Lenore. 'Will you lend me the car to drive over there? I'm going to ask him face to face.'

'Good for you. Sure you can have the car. But let me know if you're going to stay the night over there again, won't you?' Blythe said smoothly, and Lenore swung round to stare at her.

'What do you mean?' she demanded. 'Just what are you implying?'

'Nothing,' replied Blythe airily, but there was a knowing twinkle in her dark eyes. 'I don't want to spend another night worrying about you, that's all. Take care when you're driving, won't you?'

The weeks of May sunshine that had followed the late Easter snowstorm had brought about miraculous changes in the gardens of the houses along Bay Street West. Lawns had turned green. Daffodils and some tulips nodded in the sea-breeze and buds were beginning to burst into leaf on the maples and birches.

The driveway to the Jonson house was striped with gold where the sunlight shone through the branches of the pines, and the house itself seemed to glow with reflected light against the washed blue of the sky, looking very different from the last time she had seen it.

She went up the steps and rang the doorbell.

From inside the house came the sound of barking. After a while the barking stopped, but the door didn't open, so she rang again. More barking that stopped again after a while. The door didn't open.

'Adam Jonson, you can't fool me,' Lenore muttered to herself. 'I know you're in there.'

The front door wasn't locked and bolted and she was able to push it open, cautiously because she didn't want Caesar to come growling and snarling at her. Much to her surprise the dog wasn't in the hallway and she was able to step inside unhindered.

Closing the door after her quietly, she stood for a few moments listening. Compared with the last time she had stood in that hallway the house was full of light. It was also silent. No wind whined. No timbers creaked.

'Adam?' she called. 'Adam? It's me—Lenore!'

From the back of the house came the sound of the dog barking, but Caesar didn't slink into the hallway and she presumed he was shut into the kitchen. He could hear her and knew she had come in, but he couldn't do anything about it.

There was no answer to her call, so she moved towards the entrance to the big living-room. Sunlight slanted in from the west-facing windows and shone on the glass-fronted cabinets. The piano glowed rosily. The oak floor gleamed golden-brown. The pale marble of the fireplace and the silver candelabra added touches of coolness. The green velvet curtains shimmered softly. More than ever Lenore felt that the gracious and elegant room was a perfect setting for a small concert of chamber music. She could almost hear the sound of the piano and the strings playing a Brahms quartet followed by the lyrical lilt of a divertimento for woodwind and strings by Mozart, with herself playing the clarinet.

Adam wasn't in the room and there were no signs of him having been in it that day. It was neat and dusted.

'Hello. Anyone at home?' she called when she returned to the hallway. Only the dog barked again.

The door to the room that Adam used as a bedroom was closed. Was it possible he was in there? Lenore went over to it and knocked sharply, then turned the knob, pushed the door and looked in. The bed was made. The furniture shone. Adam wasn't there.

She closed the door and stood still again, listening and thinking, then went down the passage to the kitchen and knocked on that door. The dog barked in a frenzy of excitement and she could hear it pawing the other side of the door. She thumped on the door.

'Adam Jonson, are you in there?' she called.

The dog barked and barked, half crazy with frustration because it couldn't get out of the kitchen. Not daring to open the door in case Caesar jumped at her, Lenore, also feeling frustrated, began to make her way back along the passage. The barking stopped, and she looked back. The kitchen door swung open and Adam appeared, his hair ruffled, dark shades glinting, hiding his eyes, taut lips curling back from white teeth.

'My God,' he snarled, 'don't you ever give up? Why have you come here? What do you want now?'

The sight of him, tall and wide-shouldered in sweater and jeans, had the strangest effect on her. It seemed suddenly as if her legs had turned to jelly, and she put a hand against the wall to support herself.

'To . . . to see you,' she whispered. 'I've come to see you—to ask you what I was going to ask you on the phone, only—only you hung up.'

She couldn't take her eyes off him. She could only stare and stare, spellbound again. He stood very still for a few moments seeming to stare at her too. Then he moved abruptly, closing the kitchen door behind him. Shut in the kitchen, the dog whimpered at being cut off from its master.

Sunlight didn't reach that far down the passage and with the kitchen door closed there wasn't much light. Adam stepped towards her and stopped to stand in front of her. Raising a hand, he touched her face, fingertips stroking her cheek, pressing against the skin and the moulding of the cheekbone before moving on to her temple and thrusting into her hair.

'You are real, then,' he murmured strangely, peering down at her through the dark lenses while his fingers made free with silky strands of her hair, winding in it, pulling at it as if they couldn't have enough of it.

'Yes, yes, I'm real,' she said shakily. Eroticism was racing along her nerves, boiling in her blood, aroused by his touch and by his nearness. 'Oh, yes, I'm real—very real.'

And she reached out to him, her hands sliding up his chest to his shoulders, her face lifting willingly to his as he bent his head to kiss her.

CHAPTER FIVE

URGENTLY they kissed, like lovers who have long been separated, passion, white-hot, flowing freely through their mouths and from their fingertips. In that dark corner of the silent house they clung to each other and for a while had no knowledge or sense of time or place. They knew and sensed only each other.

But, as Adam pushed her back against the wall and his hands began to move intimately over the curves of her breasts under the open tweed jacket she was wearing with a blouse and skirt, Lenore struggled to surface above the waves of sensuousness which were sweeping over her.

'No, no,' she whispered, her hands curving about his wrists in an effort to stop his marauding hands. 'Wait—oh, please wait! I didn't come just for this. I came to ask you . . .'

The rest of what she had to say was cut off by the savagery of his mouth dominating hers again, and a sultry darkness seemed to take over her mind, blotting out reasonable thought. She ceased being a person, independent and in control of her own destiny, and became a creature ruled entirely by emotion and sensation, completely at the mercy of Adam's lips and hands and wanting to stay like that, glorying in his mastery, welcoming his domination as he pressed the whole length of his hard body against hers, the thrust of his hips making her aware of his arousal.

Breathlessly he whispered in her ear,

'Now I know you're real. I wasn't sure, you
see. I thought I might have dreamed you'd stayed
the night with me and slept with me. And when
you phoned this afternoon I thought I was
imagining things again. That's why I hung up.'
He laughed softly, his breath tickling the tender
skin of her ear-lobe, causing delicious shivers to
spiral through her. 'But it worked. You came
here, and now I know you're real, flesh and
blood, and not a phantom like the Lenore in the
poem.' He pushed away from her but took hold
of her arms, his fingers biting cruelly into soft
flesh. 'Why did you leave me before I woke up
that morning?' he demanded fiercely. 'Why did
you go?'

'I didn't want the Smiths to find us together,
in bed,' she replied, staring up at him, a little
frightened by his behaviour. Was he crazy after
all? Had living alone for so long frustrated by his
half-blindness, addled his brain? 'And . . . and I
had to go back to the Inn as soon as I could, to
see Blythe. It was best that I left when I did.
Don't you see that, Adam?'

'I don't *see* anything much,' he growled
bitterly. 'Best for whom? Not for me.' He jerked
her towards him again. The dark lenses glared
down at her. 'Now that you're here I'm not
letting you go like that again.'

'But you can't make me stay if I don't want to,'
she retorted.

'You'll want to—I'll make sure of that,' he said
softly, his head tipping towards hers until his lips
were a hair's breadth from her mouth, hovering
over it tormentingly, tempting her to kiss him

again. Quickly she turned her head sideways to avoid temptation.

'Please, please behave sensibly,' she whispered. 'Let's go somewhere to talk. I really came to ask a favour of you. Can we go into the living room? It's about that room I want to ask you.'

As she had hoped, mention of the room diverted him momentarily. His hands slid down her arms and he stepped back from her.

'Okay, we'll go to the living room and talk,' he agreed.

She followed him along the passage and into the long wide room with the velvet curtains and the grand piano. She sat on the sofa and he stood by the fireplace, one arm resting along the marble overmantel as he turned to face her.

'So what's this favour you want to ask,' he said abruptly.

He didn't sound very approachable now, she thought, and his mouth had a cynical twist to it. She had thought of many ways to ask him, but now that the moment had come she couldn't think of how to begin. She glanced around the room as if searching for inspiration and her gaze stayed with the piano, admiring again the sheen of its rosy wood, the elegance of its curves. It looked as if someone had been playing it, because the top was open. Her eyes widened slightly, their attention drawn to something that was resting against the piano stool—a classical guitar, a very new-looking guitar, its pale wood gleaming yellow in the sunlight. She hadn't noticed it when she had looked into the room before.

'Where did you get the guitar?' she exclaimed.

'I asked Albert to buy it for me when he was in

Bangor,' he replied coolly, then added softly, 'Your advice when you were here last made a big impression on me.'

'And have you been playing it?' she asked, turning to look at him again.

'I've been trying.'

'I'm glad,' she whispered, then hurried on, 'When I was here before did I tell you about the music group that's started up in Northport?'

'No.' He frowned. 'Are you a member of it?'

'Yes, now I am. I went to a meeting. . . .'

'If you've come to ask me to join it, forget it,' he interrupted harshly. 'I'm not going to make a fool of myself in front of other musicians.'

'I'm not going to ask you to join,' she replied spiritedly. 'They only want people who can play, really play. They already have a string quartet and a pianist and they're now ready to put on their first concert. But they can't find a suitable place to perform in.'

She paused and studied his face. Was he listening? Or was he bored, turned off? It was hard to tell.

'Anyway,' she went on, 'I told them about this room and the piano.'

'You did? Why?' Adam spoke sharply.

'Because . . . because I couldn't help thinking what a perfect setting it would be for a chamber music concert, with the piano and all. And Isaac . . . that's Isaac Goldstein, the violinist, he's retired now . . . asked me to ask you if you'd lend the room to them for their first concert.' She paused again, hesitantly seeing how hard his face had grown, then added weakly, 'So here I am asking you. Would you lend them the room, Adam, please?'

'And that's the only reason you phoned me and came here, to ask me that?' he said.

'Yes, the only reason,' she whispered.

For a few moments he didn't move, nor did he say anything. Then he moved suddenly to stride away from the fireplace across to the piano. He stood there for a while with his back to her smoothing the side of the piano with long fingers. Slowly he turned to lean within the curve of the piano. Beneath the dark glasses his mouth was set in a grim line.

'I suppose you think I owe you one for making you stay and sleep with me the other night,' he accused harshly.

'No, oh no—I don't think that at all.' Lenore sprang to her feet and went over to him. 'Really, I don't,' she added, then burst out, 'And you're hateful to believe that of me. Oh, why are you so suspicious?'

'Call it a natural cynicism where women are concerned,' he drawled nastily. 'A form of self-preservation built into most men.'

'Oh, I wish I hadn't come,' she raged helplessly. 'I wish I hadn't come! I guessed you'd be like this!' She swung away from him and made for the doorway.

'Lenore—where are you going?'

She turned back. He was coming after her. She stopped and waited until he reached her.

'I'm going back to Northport to tell the group I asked you to lend them the room and that you refused,' she snapped.

'But I haven't refused,' he replied coolly. 'Not yet. I might, just might, agree to let them give their first concert in this room. It depends a lot on you.'

'Oh? In what way?' She was surprised, and showed it by staring up at him, her eyes wide. He looked down at her, peering intently through the dark lenses.

'I've been thinking over the other advice you gave me when you stayed the night,' he told her, 'not just the bit about taking up the guitar again.'

'Wh-what advice was that?' she whispered.

'About marriage. You suggested it was something I could do. Getting married, having children would give me a reason for living, you said. Remember?'

'Yes, I remember.' Her voice was a thread of sound.

'Well, I've decided that you're right. I ought to get married, and if you'll agree to marry me as soon as we can get a licence I'll agree to let your music group perform their concerts in this room,' he said clearly and concisely.

'That's . . . it's . . . you're crazy!' she stammered, feeling stunned. 'We . . . we can't get married!'

'Why can't we? We're both adults, free to do as we like,' he retorted. 'What or who can stop us?'

'But . . . we're not . . . we don't love each other. I'm not in love with you and you're not in love with me,' she faltered.

'Then what the hell is it that's going on between us?' Adam demanded roughly, seizing hold of her arms again and jerking her towards him. 'Why do we both ignite when we meet?' he growled between set teeth.

'It . . . it isn't love. It isn't love,' Lenore cried out, her hand flat against his chest, holding him off. 'It's infatuation and it won't last. It never does, and it isn't a reason for marriage.'

'Who says so?' he demanded.

Only just in time Lenore bit back the words, 'Ann Landers says so, in her counselling column,' and felt hysterical laughter rising within her.

'I do,' she spluttered. 'I . . . I can't marry you because I . . . I don't love you.'

'You don't sound very sure,' he drawled, his mood changing again, his hands relaxing their grip of her arms to slide up to and along her shoulders to her throat. Lightly and suggestively his fingers trailed over her skin and from within her slender body came a response stronger than her will that made her moan and close her eyes in protest against such a violent turbulence.

'Marry me, Lenore, and live here with me,' he said, his breath warm on her lips. 'Marry me and you can have all the music groups in the world to play here whenever you like. Marry me and this house will be yours to do whatever you want with it. You see how generous I can be?'

'But only when you want something in return,' she whispered. 'Oh, let me go! I . . . I can't think straight when you're kissing me.' His lips were blazing a trail along the line of her jaw and across her cheek. 'Or when you're touching me.' His fingers had slid within the opening of her blouse and their cool tips were stroking the fast-hardening breast.

'So don't think,' he murmured. 'Just feel. And do what you feel you want to do and let's make the most of whatever it is that's going on between us; infatuation, spring fever, call it what you will. It's here, it's now and it's good. It's so very good.'

His lips took hers and darkness invaded her mind again; a black magic that caused her head to spin. He was right, it was good, and she longed to go all the way with him again, but a strange fear was creeping across her mind now like a cold grey light dispersing the warm heady darkness, showing up the dangers that might be in store for her if she agreed to marry him. She opened her eyes, wrenched her mouth from his and pushed him away from her.

'No, no!' she cried. 'I can't marry you. You're not normal, so I can't marry you. I'm afraid to marry you!'

'Afraid? Why, for God's sake?' His face had gone white.

'Because . . . because you have it in you to . . . to. . . .' Her voice faltered and broke.

'To what?' rasped Adam. 'What do I have it in me to do?'

But she couldn't tell him after all that he had it in him to break her heart because one day, when he had got over his fury and frustration at being incapacitated by his blindness he might regret having married her and would want his freedom again.

'Nothing, nothing!' she cried out wildly. She took a deep breath and attempted to be more controlled. 'The answer is no, Adam. I won't marry you, not even to help the music group to get the use of this room,' she added more quietly. 'I'll go now. I guess . . . I guess you won't want me to stay. Goodbye.'

She turned and walked across the room into the hallway. He didn't call after her and he didn't follow her. She opened the door and stepped out into the warm spring sunshine. Down the steps. Across to the car. Into the driver's seat. She moved like a robot, stiffly without feelings. Only a robot's hand didn't shake as hers was shaking when she turned the key in the ignition. And a robot couldn't cry salt tears as she was crying when she drove away and down the driveway.

Never had she felt like this, not even when she had parted from Herzel. She felt as if she were being torn in two. Part of her longed to go back to try and explain to Adam what she had meant when she had said she couldn't marry him because he wasn't normal; to take him in her arms and kiss him; to stay all night with him and make love with him. Yet part of her wanted to get away as far as possible, to hide in a corner somewhere until the pain of hurting him had eased; until she had forgotten him and he had forgotten her.

She shouldn't have gone to see him, she argued, as she drove along Pickering Lane. She should have listened to reason instead of impulsively obeying the desire to see him again. Then it wouldn't have happened. He wouldn't have asked her to marry him and she wouldn't have been placed in the position of having to refuse.

Oh, God, would she ever be able to forget the expression on his face when she had said she couldn't marry him because he wasn't normal? She had been cruel to be kind. She had meant that if his eyesight had been normal he would never have asked her to marry him. She had been trying to prevent him from making a mistake he might regret later. Oh, she hoped that one day he would understand and would forgive her for what she had said.

'Land sakes, what's with you?' exclaimed Blythe when Lenore walked into the kitchen at the Inn. 'You look as if the end of the world was in sight! Did you have another set-to with the lion? Did he bite after all?'

'I shouldn't have gone to see him,' Lenore muttered, collapsing on a chair at the table. 'Oh, Blythe, I made such a mess of it!' she wailed, and burst into tears.

'I guess he refused,' said Blythe dryly, and dipping the soup ladle into the big pan on the stove she scooped up some soup and tasted it. 'Was he rude?'

'Yes ... and no,' replied Lenore, sniffing. 'He ... he asked me to marry him.'

'What?' Blythe dropped the ladle into the soup and spun around to stare with rounded eyes. 'You're kidding!'

'No, I'm not.' Lenore wiped the tears from her cheeks with her knuckles. 'He said he would let the music group have the room for their concert if I would agree to marry him.'

'He must be crazy!'

'He is. He's half mad because he can't see properly and can't do the work he likes to do. That's why I said no.'

'You turned him down?'

'Of course I did. You wouldn't expect me to marry a man I hardly know, and who doesn't know what he's doing or saying, would you?'

'I guess not,' agreed Blythe. 'But I don't understand why you're so upset about it, when you don't like him.'

'I've never said I don't like him,' retorted Lenore, her eyes flashing. 'Never!'

'Maybe you haven't, but you sure behave as if you don't,' said Blythe.

'He isn't the sort of person you like or don't like. You either love him or hate him,' mused Lenore.

'Oh, really?' remarked Blythe, raising her eyebrows mockingly. 'And you hate him, I guess.'

'Oh, I don't know. I don't know!' cried Lenore. 'I don't want to talk about him any more.'

'Okay,' Blythe shrugged. 'But it's a pity you didn't get him to agree to let the music group have the room. When are you going to tell Isaac?'

'Tomorrow,' said Lenore listlessly, and no more was said about the matter.

Troubled by thoughts of Adam, of the way he had looked when she had refused his proposal, she slept badly and wakened the next morning feeling depressed and, what was worse, feeling guilty.

'You're wishing you hadn't refused, aren't you?' remarked Blythe shrewdly as they breakfasted in the kitchen. Outside, sunshine sparkled on wet grass and the robins hopped about listening for worms. Other birds were singing. Trees were bursting into leaf. Tulips, red and gold, clustered together in the flower beds.

'I couldn't do anything else but refuse,' sighed Lenore. 'I'm just wishing that I . . . that he. . . . Oh, damn!' She clutched at her head with her hands and with her elbows on the table stared down at the dish in front of her. 'I wish he hadn't asked me and then I wouldn't have had to refuse and make him think that I'd rejected him because . . . because he's half blind.'

'Mmm, I see what you mean,' said Blythe. 'It isn't a nice feeling, knowing that you might have hurt his feelings and, what's worse, struck a blow at his masculine pride. He must be hating you pretty badly this morning.'

'I guess so,' Lenore sighed miserably. She looked across the table and considered her sister's face, the oval shape of it, the creamy skin, the placid doe-like eyes. Unlike herself Blythe always seemed to be so much in control of her life. She didn't get passionately involved with anyone. 'Blythe, have you ever been infatuated with a man?' she asked.

'Infatuated?' Blythe's eyebrows went up in surprise and she smiled, her slow half-mocking smile. 'What do you mean?'

'I guess the definition of the word would be to feel crazy about a person you hardly know, on . . . on a physical level.' Lenore felt the blood burn in her cheeks suddenly. Even though Blythe was her sister they had never before discussed sexual matters, both of them feeling that the subject was strictly personal.

'Inspired with extravagant passion, affected with extreme folly—I think that's the dictionary definition of the word,' mused Blythe, still smiling a little as she studied the coffee in her mug. 'Yes, I've felt like that, once or twice, when I was younger.' She looked up suddenly, her smile fading, her dark eyes hardening. 'You feel like that about Adam Jonson?' she asked sharply.

'Yes . . . at least I think so. It can't be anything

else but infatuation, because I don't know him well enough to be in love with him. It . . . it's the same with him.'

'Good God!' whispered Blythe. 'But you haven't . . . surely you haven't. . . .'

'Made love with him?' put in Lenore, her cheeks burning hotter than ever. 'Yes,' she confessed. 'The night of the storm . . . and then again yesterday . . . we . . . we could hardly keep our hands off each other . . .'

'Oh no!' groaned Blythe. 'Lenore, how could you let him take advantage of you like that?'

'But that's what I'm trying to tell you. He didn't take advantage, because I wanted to do it too. Oh, we both fought against it and each other . . . but in the end we couldn't help it. It . . . it was stronger than we were.'

'Then why have you refused to marry him?'

'For that reason. Can't you see? Infatuation doesn't last. It isn't a good basis for marriage.'

'Ann Landers again,' mocked Blythe, her mouth twisting. 'But if it's only infatuation he's feeling too why do you think he asked you to marry him?'

'Because—oh, because I suggested to him when we were talking once that marriage was something he could do even though he was half blind. I said it to . . . well, to sort of comfort him, because he was really down about the latest diagnosis about his sight, feeling really helpless and useless. He's only asked me to marry him because I happen to be the one woman he's come into contact with for a while.'

'And because he's attracted to you,' said Blythe firmly. 'In spite of what the so-called marriage counsellors say, physical attraction is a very important part of a relationship, and most love affairs, most marriages begin like that. You see someone across a room and he sees you and *wham*, if the chemistry is right, it begins.' She paused, then added very quietly, 'At least it was like that with Josh and me.'

Lenore stared in surprise at her sister's down-bent head, at the straight white centre parting in the thick black hair.

'Where ... where did you meet him?' she asked, glad to be able to direct the course of the conversation away from herself and Adam.

'At a yard sale, last spring.'

'A yard sale?' exclaimed Lenore, memories of visiting yard sales with her father when they had been on vacation in Maine years ago flooding into her mind. Mainers were noted for their yard sales. Every year they cleared out their attics and their garages and their basements and put the stuff they found in their yards, as their gardens were called, and invited everyone to come and buy. Sometimes it was possible to pick up genuine antiques for a few dollars. Her father had had a good eye for jewellery and had found many a good silver chain or gold brooch hiding amongst the clutter of ugly costume jewellery and had sold the pieces later for a good price.

'Yes. It was up at the Simmonds' house. You remember the place, up river? The old lady, Marsha Simmonds, who used to live there, died. There were no heirs to the estate, so the executors of her will put it up for sale. Most of the good furniture went to the auction rooms, but some of the stuff from the kitchen and servants' quarters was put out in the biggest yard sale ever known in these parts.' Blythe pointed to the chairs set about the table. 'These chairs came from that sale. Josh went up there to look for wood, preferably oak, to use for finishing boats. He bought a huge oak table for a few dollars.'

'You saw each other at a yard sale and *wham*, the chemistry began to work. Is that how it was, do you say?'

'That's right. It wasn't quite as explosive as your meetings with Adam Jonson, but then neither Josh nor I are very dynamic people. It was slow. It's still slow.' Blythe paused, an expression of pain flitting across her face. 'You see, he's married.'

'Oh, Blythe!' whispered Lenore.

'He's been separated from his wife for nearly three years now. It happened when ... when he bought the boatyard here. She wouldn't come—didn't like the idea of living in a country place, it seems. Didn't like him giving up his job in Boston and becoming a boatbuilder, I guess.'

'Then why doesn't he divorce her?'

'She ... she won't agree to a divorce. She's still hoping his business here will fail and he'll want to go back to Boston. Oh, it's a most unpleasant situation, Lenore. I don't like saying this about another woman, but she really is a bitch. She doesn't want to do anything to help Josh. She isn't being a real wife to him, but she won't let him go.'

'Are there any children?'

'No, thank God.' Blythe finished drinking her coffee and stood up. 'Time I started work. I'm catering a birthday party for tonight—a big one.

Northport's oldest inhabitant, Tom Elder, is ninety-five today and his family and friends are putting on the party. I hope you'll be around to help. What are you going to do this morning?'

'Go and see Isaac, I guess, and tell him the bad news about not getting the loan of Adam Jonson's living room for the concert,' said Lenore with a sigh.

'If you like you can offer the music group the use of the lounge here. It's not a bad size. You could put a grand piano in the front window alcove and I could arrange seating for about fifty people if I took the sofas and armchairs out. We could also put on a reception for that first concert. You know, wine and cheese, so that the audience can meet the performers. I wouldn't charge them anything because it would be good publicity for the Inn, especially if you get coverage of the concert by the local TV station.'

'Blythe, you're an angel!' Lenore hugged her sister. 'I'll tell Isaac—it will be just enough to take the edge off his disappointment. I feel much better now. Thank you, thank you!'

'Confession is always good for the soul,' remarked Blythe dryly, referring indirectly to Lenore's confession that she was suffering from infatuation for Adam and had made love with him. 'But don't mind me. I guess I'm just envious because you ... and Adam both recognised what it was you wanted from each other and did something about it. At least you had some rapture together; something good to remember. Do you want the car to go to Isaac's house?'

'No. I think I can walk that far. My knee is much better,' said Lenore. 'It isn't far.'

In the small garden enclosed by a white picket fence in front of Isaac's house, bushes of forsythia blazed yellow. On the black front door the brass knocker, shaped like an American bald eagle, shone brightly. Lenore knocked twice and the door was opened immediately by Rose Goldstein, small and white-haired, dressed in pants and a loose overblouse.

'Isaac was just thinking of phoning you,' she said, standing back to let Lenore step into the house. 'Isaac,' she called, 'Lenore is here!'

Isaac came bustling out of the living room. His face was wreathed in smiles and he came towards her with both hands outstretched and took hold of her hands and raised them to his lips.

'You did it. You did it!' he exclaimed excitedly.

'Did what?' queried Lenore, bewildered by this expression of joy.

'You bearded the formidable lion, Adam Jonson, in his lair and got him to agree to let us use his house for our concert!'

'I did?' said Lenore faintly.

'But of course. Isn't that why you're here, to tell me that?'

'Now, Isaac, calm down, calm down and take Lenore through to the living room. I'll put on the coffee pot. You like coffee in the morning, Lenore?' said the practical Rose.

'Yes, yes,' said Lenore, as she was tugged by the effervescent Isaac into the pretty oak-beamed living room. Isaac pushed her into one of the chintz-covered armchairs and sat down on an old Windsor-backed rocking chair.

'First thing this morning, he phoned me,' said Isaac. 'It was just after seven, and Rose and I were still in bed. He said you'd asked him yesterday and that overnight he'd considered the request and had decided to let us have the use of the two big rooms on the ground floor of his house for the concert. He wants me—and anyone else belonging to the music group—to go to the house this afternoon to look at the room. By then he hopes to have contacted the local public television network to send a producer and cameraman to meet us and to view the room we want to use so they can plan how to film the concert.' Isaac paused for breath and clapped his hands together excitedly. 'It's wonderful, just wonderful! I can hardly believe it, and it's all thanks to you.'

Lenore could hardly believe it either.

'I didn't know, I didn't think . . . when I left him yesterday afternoon I had no idea he would agree,' she whispered. 'In fact I got the impression that he would refuse.'

'So?' Isaac's eyes twinkled. 'Perhaps he teased you a little, eh? Perhaps he pretends he's not interested so he can surprise you today. Some people are like that when they find themselves in a position of power. He expects us to go around four o'clock this evening—that's when Jack can come with us. Also I ask Willa to come with us. Jack must see the piano, you see, and Willa is good on acoustics and that sort of thing.'

'I won't come,' said Lenore firmly. 'You won't want me there.'

'But of course you must go,' said Rose, coming into the room with a tray of coffee mugs. 'You're the public relations member of the group. You made the contact with Mr Jonson. Isaac, insist that she go with you to introduce you to Mr Jonson.'

'I insist that you come, Lenore,' said Isaac, his eyes twinkling more than ever with amusement. 'Me, I'm very shy, as Rose will tell you. If you won't come with me I don't go, and we lose this chance to have our concert in that house.'

'You might find that the room isn't suitable after all,' suggested Lenore, taking a proffered mug of coffee from Rose.

'I do not know that until I see it,' retorted Isaac. 'And I do not see it if you do not come with me.'

'Oh, all right, I'll come with you. But I must come back before six, to help Blythe. She's catering a birthday party for Mr Elder.'

'You'll be back for then, I promise,' replied Isaac. 'And now I wish to ask you if you would be good enough to play with us at the concert. Jack and I have decided that now we have a clarinettist who plays with such a pure tone we would like to perform with you. Would you agree to doing the trio for clarinet, viola and piano in E flat major by Mozart? It would make a good evening of music with the Brahms.'

'I'd love to,' agreed Lenore enthusiastically, and immediately forgot all her qualms about going to the Jonson house that afternoon and having to see Adam again.

'But why? Why would he do this?' she said to Blythe later, after telling her sister that Adam had agreed to let the music group use his house for the concert. 'He said he would only agree to do it if I agreed to marry him, and I didn't.'

'Don't ask me,' retorted Blythe. 'Ask him when you see him again this afternoon.'

'I tried to get out of going, but Isaac insisted I go—said he wouldn't go if I wouldn't,' sighed Lenore.

'Why don't you want to go?'

'I don't want to see Adam again, of course. Oh, Blythe, I'm afraid of him—really afraid,' she whispered.

'Afraid he might come on strong again and you won't be able to resist?' guessed Blythe shrewdly.

'Yes, that's it exactly,' admitted Lenore.

'Then you'll just have to make sure you don't find yourself alone with him for longer than half an hour, won't you,' replied Blythe dryly. 'Stay close to Isaac. I guess he'll be delighted to protect you.'

'It isn't funny!' flared Lenore.

'No, I suppose it isn't. But feeling the way you do, I can't understand why you turned down his proposal.'

'I don't want to be married just because I seem to be . . . available,' retorted Lenore. 'I . . . I want to be married for . . . for love.'

'Don't we all?' sighed Blythe. 'But how often does that happen? See you later.'

There was a smell of newly-mown grass in the air when Lenore stepped out of Isaac's car at four o'clock that afternoon, and Albert Smith was riding round the big lawn beside the house on a small grass-cutting tractor. Beyond the edge of the green slope the bay glittered with afternoon sunlight, islands seeming to float on its surface, and in the distance the hills were misty purple against the sun-bright blue of the sky.

'Beautiful. Beautiful!' exclaimed Isaac, clapping his hands in delight.

The house was in mellow mood, windows winking with light, clapboard gleaming softly. The front door was open and Lenore led the way into the hallway. From the doorway on the right led the way into the hall. From the living room came the sound of voices. She went over to the doorway and stepped into the room. Adam was standing by the piano. Two people were with him, a woman and a man. The woman, who was casually dressed in brown slacks, a white blouse and a brown tweed short jacket with a brightly coloured scarf tied around her neck, had a thin elfin face and a lot of curly brown hair. She noticed Lenore and said something to Adam. He swung round to face the door.

'Adam.' Lenore stepped forward nervously. Wearing a thin sweater and dark blue jeans, he seemed bigger and tougher than ever and the dark glasses gave his lightly suntanned face a sort of supercilious expression. 'Isaac Goldstein is here with Jack Kenata and Willa Caplan,' she went on as coolly as she could. 'May they come in and look at the room?'

He stiffened at the sound of her voice and frowned and she thought for a moment that he wasn't going to answer her. Then he said coldly,

'Of course they can come in. That's why they've come, isn't it, to look at the room?'

But his manner changed miraculously as soon as she introduced Isaac. No longer frigidly stiff, he shook the violinist's hand warmly, and he was just as welcoming towards Jack and Willa. Then he introduced the other two people.

The woman was Valerie Brown, who was a producer of programmes for the local public broadcasting network, and the young man was Jim Lorway who would film the concert.

'Now please feel free to look around and to discuss with Val and Jim what it is you want to do,' Adam added. 'And if there's anything you want to ask me you'll find me outside on the terrace.'

Smoothly polite, coolly autocratic, he was very different from the Adam she knew, thought Lenore, as she watched him leave the room through one of the long open windows. And he had ignored her. She might as well have not been there.

She hardly heard what Isaac was saying to the two from the TV network. The urge to follow Adam from the room was too strong, and she gave in to it, excusing herself and walking across to the open window, pretending she didn't know that they had all turned to watch her leave the room.

Adam was at the far end of the terrace and seemed to be staring at the view of green land sloping down to blue water, distant islands and hills, and although the heels of her sandals clicked on the stone flags of the terrace and he must have heard her approaching him, he didn't turn towards her.

'Adam,' she said when she was close to him.

'Why have you come?' he snapped the words at her and bone showed white at the corner of his jaw as he gritted his teeth.

'Isaac insisted that I came with him to introduce him to you,' she replied rather breathlessly. Being near to him again was causing that silly weakness to flow through her. She wanted to put her arms around him, lean against him. She wanted to feel his arms about her, his lips against her cheek, his fingers at her breast. Oh, how she wanted him! 'Adam, why did you agree to let the group have the room?' she rushed on, looking away from him at the view. It was safer to look that way than at him. Much safer. 'I hope it wasn't ... well, I hope you're not expecting me to change my mind and agree to marry you just because you've done this for them.'

'I'm expecting nothing from you,' he said in the same hard frostbitten tones. 'Nothing at all. You're the type that blows hot, then blows cold. One minute you're offering everything you've got, the next you're wanting back what you've given. You're an Indian giver.'

'I'm not!' she flared. 'Oh, how can you say that? How can you pass judgement on me like that when you hardly know me?'

'I know enough!' He almost spat the words at her. 'And I don't want to know any more.' He drew a deep breath as if to assert control over himself and went on more quietly, 'I offered the use of the room to Isaac Goldstein and his music group because I happen to have great respect for him as a person and a musician. I also think it's a good thing for the community of Northport to have such a cultural event held here. My decision to let them use the room had nothing to do with you.'

Silence, but not complete, for there was the sound of the tractor, the singing of birds, and from the room behind him the bitter-sweet music of a Chopin Nocturne being played on the piano by Jack Kanata. Lenore, hearing the romantic music, felt as if her heart was being squeezed.

'Adam, I'm sorry,' she began softly. 'I . . .'

'For turning down my proposal?' he asked, turning on her, his lips taut and bitter. 'Don't be. You were right to refuse. I wasn't normal when I made it. I was out of my mind, and I want you to forget it. I want you to consider it was never made. Okay?'

Eyes wide and glistening suddenly with unshed tears, Lenore gazed up at the dark glasses that glared down at her, wishing not for the first time that she could see his eyes, gauge his real feelings from them. Surely he didn't mean what he was saying? Surely he wasn't as cruel as the savage set of his lips suggested?

'But I don't . . .' she began, and he cut in sharply.

'And don't come here again—by yourself, I mean. Don't ever come here unless you're with someone. I don't want you here by yourself. Stay away from me. Understand?'

'But if Isaac and the group decide the room is suitable for the concert I'll have to come again. You see, Isaac has asked me to perform with them at the concert,' she retorted. 'And I want to. I'm not going to back out now just because you don't want me here.'

'You won't be alone if you're with them, will you?' Adam pointed out dryly, his lips twisting.

'I guess I won't.' She couldn't see the view any more, because her eyes had filled with tears again. 'Adam . . .' she began, turning to him appealingly, but broke off and stepped back a pace when he swore viciously at her.

'Don't argue with me!' he grated. 'Don't say any more. It's over, done with. Forget it.'

He stepped past her and strode away along the terrace. The piano had stopped, and Lenore could hear voices. Her few moments alone with him were over. The affair with him, that flare-up of white-hot passion, was over. Done with, he had said. Before her eyes the flowing green land and the glittering blue sea blurred as she struggled to control an overwhelming desire to fling herself down on the ground and to sob and beat at the ground with her fists.

'Isaac tells me it's thanks to you that Adam has agreed to let the music ensemble perform in his house.'

The voice was female and rather harsh; abrasive, the voice of a woman accustomed to giving orders and having them obeyed. Valerie Baker. Lenore stiffened but didn't turn immediately. She had to get rid of the teardrops that had spilled on to her cheeks first, stroking them away with a forefinger.

'I was merely the go-between,' she muttered, then turned and attempted a smile. 'There usually has to be one,' she added, 'between two people who don't know each other and have never met.'

'How long have you known Adam?' asked Valerie. Now that she was close Lenore could see that the other woman was older than herself, around thirty-five, about Adam's age. 'As far as I can remember he's never spoken of you to me,' Valerie continued, 'and I've known him a long time.'

'How long?' asked Lenore. A new feeling was

surging up in her; an ugly feeling that had a sour taste to it. Jealousy of this cool self-confident woman who had known Adam a long time?

'Oh, about ten years. We started our careers in television at the same network about the same time.'

'Oh, I didn't know. I've only known him since I came here about two or three weeks ago, I guess. I'm not sure. We met by accident. Have you visited him here before? I mean, did you know he'd come to live here?' asked Lenore.

'Sure I knew he was living here.' Valerie laughed a little and her eyes, which were catlike, hazel-yellow shot with green sparks and slanted upward at the outer corners, sparkled. 'I lived with him here for a few weeks before Christmas.'

'Oh, then you're the woman who . . .' Lenore began, realised she was about to be indiscreet and stopped.

'The woman who what?' demanded Valerie sharply, her amusement fading, her eyes narrowing and becoming even more catlike. 'Adam has said something about me to you?'

'No. My sister . . . she owns the Northport Inn . . . told me that there was a woman living here for a while. She used to see you in the village. Then you went away, she said,' replied Lenore vaguely, remembering vividly Albert Smith's caustic remarks about Valerie and how she had come to leave. A bitch, he had called her, and there had been a dust-up between Adam and Valerie, so the woman had left.

'I didn't go far,' replied Valerie, with a wry twist to her lips. 'When I heard he'd been badly hurt and blinded I gave up my job in New York to come and be with Adam,' she went on in a low voice. 'I did my best to help him get over the frustration that being half blind caused, but he wouldn't let me help. He's so damned proud.' She sighed heavily and her thin face took on a sad expression. 'We used to be close, he and I,' she confessed, 'very close. Whenever he was home . . . that is in New York . . . between assignments, we would get together, and I kind of hoped that one day our relationship would become permanent. I came here to be with him, but it didn't work out quite the way I hoped.' She shrugged her shoulders. 'I managed to get a job with the local public television network, and naturally when I heard there was a possibility of producing a programme in Adam's house I jumped at the chance of coming here again and seeing him.' Valerie sighed again. 'And maybe, just maybe he'll ask me to come back and live with him again.'

'Yes, maybe,' agreed Lenore. She was beginning to feel all tight inside, like an overstrung violin or guitar. Any moment now a string would break. Was the return of Valerie the reason Adam wanted her to forget his proposal of marriage? Was he glad Valerie had come back into his life? And was that why he didn't want her to come to the house any more? 'Is it all arranged, then? Have you fixed up with Isaac and Jack about the filming of the concert?' she asked, wrenching her thoughts away from personal feelings.

'No, not yet. But we're going to meet again, tomorrow, at Isaac's house. You see, I have this great idea that we do more than one concert. A series of four, I thought, each one to be filmed during the summer months in this house and then shown on TV in the fall and winter months. What do you think?' Valerie was suddenly the TV producer, crisp and determined, knowing what she wanted and how to go about achieving it.

'Sounds great. Isaac will be pleased,' said Lenore. She glanced at her watch. She had a sudden urge to run away, to get as far away as she could from Adam's house and this woman who had once been Adam's mistress and who wanted to be Adam's wife. 'I must go and find Isaac. It's time we were going back to Northport,' she murmured. 'Excuse me.' She began to walk towards one of the open windows of the living room.

'I guess I'll be seeing you again,' said Valerie, following her, 'at rehearsals for the concert. Isaac has agreed to let me come to some of them to get an idea of how you'll all look when you're playing. And then I'll want to do interviews with the players that will be shown during the intermission of the concert. You know the sort of thing—where you learned to play your instrument, your professional life to date, what your plans are for the future.'

'Oh, but I'll only be appearing for this first concert,' said Lenore as they entered the living room.

'Doesn't matter. I'd still like to interview you,' replied Valerie. 'Why won't you be here for the summer?'

Lenore glanced around the room. Adam was sitting in his favourite winged chair. Isaac and Jack were sitting on the sofa facing him and Willa was crouched on a footstool. They had been listening while Isaac talked, but he stopped when she and Valerie approached.

'I won't be here because after the first concert I'll be leaving Northport,' Lenore announced loudly and clearly for Adam's benefit. 'I'm hoping to go to Caracas, in Venezuela. I've been auditioned for a job in an orchestra out there.' She looked across at Isaac. 'Isaac, please can we go now? I promised Blythe I'd be back at the Inn at six to help her.'

'It's time we were on our way too, Val,' said Jim Lorway, appearing in the doorway from the hallway. 'I was just looking for you.'

'You go on without me, Jim,' Valerie replied, lingering by Adam. She touched his shoulder. 'Adam and I are old friends and I'd like to stay and talk with him.'

Adam stood up suddenly so that her hand was shaken off his shoulder.

'It's been a great pleasure meeting you, Isaac,' he said, shaking hands with the violinist. 'And you too.' He shook hands with Jack and Willa, then turned to Lenore. 'Goodbye,' he said coolly and firmly, but he didn't offer his hand to her.

'Goodbye,' she whispered, and turning away from him she led the others from the room into the hallway, leaving him alone with Valerie Baker.

CHAPTER SIX

'LETTER for you!' Blythe sang out as she walked into Lenore's bedroom at the Inn one morning ten days later. Lenore was sitting at the small writing desk in front of the window, but she wasn't writing. She was cleaning her clarinet in preparation for the last rehearsal before the concert, which would take place at the Jonson house on the evening of the next day, the first day of June.

'Oh, great! I hope it's about that audition for the orchestra in Caracas,' said Lenore as she drew the fluffy cleaning brush that was attached to a long cord through the core of the clarinet.

'It isn't. It's from Israel. From Herzel Rubin, in fact,' said Blythe, putting the letter down on the table. 'Have you been writing to him?'

'I sent a letter to him just before I came here, to let him know where to write if he wanted to,' replied Lenore, glancing up rather defensively. 'After all, we're still friends, Herzel and I.'

'Oh, sure,' mocked Blythe, sitting down on the edge of the bed. 'Going to open it and read it?'

'While you're here?'

'Right. I want to know what it's like living in Jerusalem.'

'He's not in Jerusalem. He's in Tel Aviv,' retorted Lenore, slitting open the envelope. 'Are you sure there wasn't anything else in the mail for me?'

'Sure I'm sure. You're really anxious about getting another job, aren't you?'

'Of course I am. I can't stay here for ever, sponging on you.'

'You wouldn't be sponging if you stayed, you'd better believe it,' retorted Blythe. 'I'd make you work if you stayed. It's going to be a busy summer, from the look of the bookings I've got so far, and I'm going to have to hire extra help if you leave. Why don't you stay at least until the end of August? Now that you're a member of the music ensemble you have plenty of opportunity to play, so you don't need to be in an orchestra. I'd have thought, knowing you, that you'd prefer being in an ensemble to being in an orchestra. It's more free, a much more personal expression.'

'You're right, it is. And I love it. But I have to eat,' argued Lenore, pulling the thick wad of folded flimsy airmail paper from the envelope. It looked as if Herzel had written a book!

'I've told you, you can work here and eat,' retorted Blythe.

'For the summer, you said. You wouldn't want me here in the winter when you're not so busy. You couldn't afford me.'

'Sure I could. I have to employ someone to help me since I keep the Inn open all winter. Why not my own sister?'

'No,' Lenore shook her head. 'It's good of you, Blythe, and don't think I don't appreciate your offer. But I couldn't stay here. I have to go— soon, too. Next week if possible.'

Lenore opened the letter to the first page. Blythe continued to sit on the bed watching Lenore's face as she read, the amused lift of the finely-plucked slanting dark eyebrows, the twitch of the full passionate lips. After a while she said, 'So what does he say?'

'He likes being there. Likes the climate, likes working in the orchestra, being with his own people, living in a *kibbutz*,' answered Lenore. Paper rustled as she turned to the third page, and her eyebrows slanted down in a frown as she read. 'Heavens!' she exclaimed. 'He wants me to go out there!'

'To play in the orchestra?'

'I wouldn't think so. Only Jewish musicians are hired, I think.' Lenore read on. 'He says he misses me and wishes we hadn't broken up. He says we could live together out there.'

'He's not offering to marry you, though?' asked Blythe.

'No. He'll never ask me to marry him, not unless I change my religion,' said Lenore.

'And would you?'

'No, not now.' She shuffled the papers together. 'Oh, Herzel, Herzel you're too late, you're too late,' she muttered.

'What do you mean, he's too late?' asked Blythe.

'I'm not in love with him any more and I don't want to live with him. I've got over it.' Lenore crammed the letter into the envelope.

'Have you?' Blythe's eyebrows tilted sardonically. 'Then why aren't you looking better? Why aren't you putting on weight? Why are you so strung up? You're in a far worse state than when you came!'

'I've had a lot on my mind,' replied Lenore. 'Practising for the concert. Rehearsing with Isaac isn't easy, you know. He's such a perfectionist. And then I'm really anxious about getting another orchestral job. The competition is keen, very keen, and orchestras are folding everywhere because of financial losses and cut-backs in government grants and subsidies.'

'All the more reason why you should consider seriously staying here, earning your bread working for me and playing for the Northport Ensemble. Who knows, this series of concerts might be so successful the ensemble will be in demand to put on more concerts, and Jack Kanata might be able to start that summer music school and festival and you could teach at that.' Blythe slid off the bed and stood up. 'What time did you say that woman was coming today to interview you?'

'Eleven o'clock.'

'Well, it's nearly that now, so I suggest you start making yourself look presentable. I presume you don't wish to be interviewed in that old dressing gown with your hair all wild and woolly.'

'No, I don't,' exclaimed Lenore, jumping to her feet as she remembered Valerie Baker's casual chic. 'What shall I wear?—oh, what shall I wear? Help me, Blythe!' She flung open the wardrobe door.

'What you usually wear for practice and rehearsal, I guess,' said Blythe. 'Why not those black slacks with a frilly blouse—the crimson one, I think. Red looks good on you and it photographs well. And pile your hair up on top of your head to show off your neck. And wear plenty of make-up to cover up those lines under your eyes, for God's sake. You haven't been sleeping well, have you?'

'Not really,' mumbled Lenore, who had discarded her dressing robe and was pulling on tailored black pants.

'And my guess it isn't just the concert or looking for a job that's keeping you awake,' said Blythe, sliding the crimson silk blouse off its hanger. 'My guess is you've got a man on your mind, and if that man isn't Herzel Rubin he's Adam Jonson! You're sorry you turned him down, aren't you?'

'No, it isn't that,' muttered Lenore as she took the blouse and began to slip her arms into the sleeves. 'Oh, I don't know what it is. I can't stop thinking about him . . . when I'm not busy, that is. He seems to fill my mind. He haunts me. I don't seem to be able to do what he told me to do.'

'And what did he tell you to do?'

'He told me to forget he'd ever proposed to me and. . . .' Lenore's lips trembled as she looked down to watch her fingers fastening the blouse. 'He told me to stay away from him,' she added in a whisper. Never would she get over the wound Adam's words had inflicted on her sensitivity. 'I've stayed away,' she went on, 'but I . . . I don't seem to be able to forget. Not while I'm here.' She raised dark anguished eyes to Blythe's compassionate face. 'So you see now why I have to go away after the concert?'

'Yes, I see,' agreed Blythe. 'I warned you, didn't I, warned you you'd soon fall in love again. Oh, Lenore, whatever am I to do with you? You can't go on like this—you must see that. You can't go on falling in and out of love all the time with totally unsuitable men. You'll have to try and control your feelings somehow.'

'Then perhaps I should get me to a nunnery, like Hamlet told Ophelia,' said Lenore dryly as she began to pin her hair up. 'That's the only place where I won't see any men, and the last place I'd find anyone like Adam Jonson!'

Ten minutes later she stepped into the lounge to find Valerie Baker and Jim Lorway already there setting up the camera and lights for filming the interview. Since their first meeting at Adam's house she had met Valerie several times at rehearsals, but they had not talked privately. This morning the TV producer was dressed in a suit of fine cream-coloured tweed which had a straight skirt and a short loose jacket under which she wore a plain linen blouse the same colour as the tweed. As usual, about her neck she had tied a colourful scarf in a cheeky knot. She looked what she was, competent and efficient, completely in charge of the situation.

'We'll talk for about twenty minutes and later I'll edit the interview, take out of it what I think is suitable to fit in with the other interviews that I've done with Isaac and Jack, Willa and Douglas. I'd like you to sit on this couch here with that painting of a sailing yacht behind you and I'll sit here beside you. Have you ever been interviewed for a TV programme before?'

'No.' Lenore sat down in the corner of the pink-covered couch and Jim came forward to clip the tiny microphone to her blouse.

'Then just relax and try to be as normal as possible,' said Valerie briskly, settling herself down and pinning a microphone on herself. 'First of all, I'll ask you why you chose to play the clarinet, then why you came to Northport and became involved with the ensemble, and lastly what your feelings are about the piece of music you're going to play. Just answer me as if you were talking to someone you know well and say as much as you want. The more you talk the better—I'm just asking the questions to get you going. Okay?'

'Okay,' Lenore nodded. 'Should I look at the camera?'

'No, look at me. The camera will be facing you anyway and will pick up all your expressions. Afterwards, since we have only one camera, we'll pretend to do the interview again with me asking the questions so that Jim can film my face while I'm speaking. Later it will all be put together at the studio. Ready to start now?'

The camera lights were hot and bright, shining directly on her face and giving the impression that the day was sunny even though she knew it was cloudy and raining outside. Once she had answered Valerie's first question about how she had chosen to be a musician Lenore found it much easier to answer the second question about why she was in Northport and how she had met Isaac and the other members of the music ensemble. But she was unprepared for the next question.

Her catlike eyes narrow yet bright with malice, Valerie smiled just a little as she spoke.

'Now I'm told that it's thanks to you that the ensemble has been allowed to perform in the beautiful eighteenth-century music room of the

Jonson house, that you have a close friendship with the owner of the house, Adam Jonson. Is this true?'

'I have met Mr Jonson, yes,' replied Lenore cautiously, but she was unable to prevent hot colour from rushing into her cheeks and her hands twisted nervously on her lap.

'Only once?' Valerie's eyebrows lifted in mock surprise.

'No ... er ... we've met more than once.' Lenore suddenly lost her temper. 'Look, I don't see what this has to do with your interview of me. I thought you wanted to know how I felt about ... about the music and not ... well, not about my ... my....'

'Your relationship with Adam?' suggested Valerie, still mocking.

'I don't have a relationship with him,' flared Lenore, and turned towards Jim Lorway. 'Is this still being taped?' she demanded.

'Sure is,' he answered from behind the camera.

'Then I'm not staying any longer to say anything else!' she snapped, springing to her feet. Finding herself entangled by the lead attached to her microphone, she unhooked the small object from her blouse and flung it down on the couch. 'And if you dare to show that part of the interview with me on TV I'll ... I'll sue you!' she added, glaring down at Valerie.

'So it's true,' drawled the producer, who was still smiling a little as she looked down at the notebook on her lap.

'What is?' demanded Lenore warily.

'You and Adam have had an affair.' Valerie looked up suddenly and Lenore stepped back a pace, alarmed by the glittering hostility in the green-flecked eyes.

'Look, if you two are going to have a fight I'm going for a smoke,' drawled Jim, who had switched off the lights and the video-tape machine. He walked out of the room into the hallway, and Valerie rose smoothly to her feet to face the scarlet-cheeked Lenore.

'What have you done to him?' she whispered. 'What have you done to Adam?'

'I ... I haven't done anything to him,' exclaimed Lenore in bewilderment. 'I don't know what you're talking about.'

'Oh, come on now, don't play the innocent with me,' jeered Valerie. 'You got at him in some way, made fun of him, perhaps. Told him that his semi-blindness was making him crazy, suggested to him that he wasn't normal.'

Lenore couldn't help stiffening. Valerie noticed, and her eyes narrowed even more, while her mouth twisted.

'So it was you,' she drawled. 'Well, I hope your conscience is strong enough to carry the burden.'

'What burden? Oh, please will you talk straight? Will you stop talking in innuendoes!' cried Lenore. 'Has something happened to Adam?' She remembered suddenly and vividly Adam threatening to shoot himself if she didn't stay the night with him, and her cheeks went as white as they had been red, a complete withdrawal of colour which left her face looking haggard and haunted. 'He hasn't ... he hasn't. . . .' she began, and broke off, because her throat closed up and her lips went dry, making it impossible for her to speak.

'Yes, he's decided to go through with the operation,' said Valerie flatly.

'Wh-what operation?' Lenore gasped, her legs suddenly giving way so that she sank down on the couch.

'Do you mean to say you didn't know?' exclaimed Valerie, frowning at her. 'Didn't he ever tell you?'

'No, not about an operation. Only ... only about how he came to be half blind. I told you we ... we met only three times. We ... we hardly know each other. What sort of operation? What will it do?'

'A very delicate operation to remove the pressure that's causing the blindness. An operation with only a sixty-forty chance of success. Sixty against Adam surviving it, because it's so delicate. One slip of the surgeon's hand and his brain will be damaged completely, or he'll die. Twice the operation has been suggested to him and twice he's refused. Now, suddenly, he's very determined to have it done because someone, and I guess it was you, has said he's not normal.' Valerie paused, her breath hissing through her teeth as she drew it in, then she leaned forward. 'If Adam dies it will be your fault,' she said in a cold hate-laden voice. 'Somehow you've got to stop him from going to New York. Go today to see him.'

'But ... but he told me to stay away from him. He told me not to go and see him again,' muttered Lenore miserably.

'So I'll leave it with you,' said Valerie coolly. 'Have a nice day,' she remarked ironically. 'It's time Jim and I went over to the Caplans' house to interview Willa. See you tomorrow at the concert.'

She went out into the hallway and a few seconds later returned with Jim to help him pack and pick up the video equipment. Lenore left the room and went up to her bedroom and closed the door. She sat for a long time thinking over what Valerie had told her, wondering if it was true. There was only one way to find out—go to see Adam and ask him.

In a few minutes she was dashing down the stairs again, wearing a zipped waterproof jacket over her blouse. Valerie and Jim had left, much to her relief, and she hurried into the kitchen where Blythe was working as usual.

'Please can I borrow the car?' she asked breathlessly. 'I'm not going far, and I won't be long.'

'Keys are in the usual place,' replied Blythe placidly. 'How did the interview go?'

'It was a disaster,' replied Lenore, taking the keys from the hook where Blythe always hung them. 'Valerie Baker and I got into a fight and Jim stopped filming us.'

'A fight? About what?' exclaimed Blythe.

'My . . . well, my friendship, if you can call it that, with Adam Jonson.'

'She's jealous?'

'You can say that again! See you later.'

The scent of newly blossoming lilacs was strong in the damp air. Soft grey rain blurred the view of sea and islands and the house on Pickering Point looked grey too and somehow withdrawn. Lenore ran up the front steps and rang the bell.

Her heart was beating with excitement and the impulsive urge that had sent her hurrying to see Adam was still pulsing through her. She didn't question that impulse. She had to see him alone before he went away to New York. She had no hope of stopping him from having the operation, but she had to see him again, be with him again before he left in case—her thoughts swerved wildly away from the dread possibility, but she forced them back on track and made herself face up to reality—she had to see him again in case he died while he was having the operation.

The door opened a crack and Bertha Smith looked out.

'Well?' she said.

'Mr Jonson—I've come to see him,' said Lenore.

'He ain't here.'

'Oh. He hasn't ... he hasn't gone away already, has he?'

'I dunno where he's gone. Went off with Albert in the truck somewhere. They're always going off together.'

'Do you know when they'll be back?' asked Lenore.

'Nope. They didn't tell me and I didn't ask. I know better than to ask either of them.'

'You don't suppose they ... they've gone to New York?' asked Lenore.

'I tell yer I dunno know where they've gone. That all you want?' Bertha was beginning to close the door.

'Yes, I guess it is. Thanks,' muttered Lenore.

The door closed and she went slowly down the steps, the desire to see Adam dissolving into disappointment and then into something very close to despair. He'd gone and she would never see him again, she was sure, for if the operation was successful and he recovered his sight he would never come here again. He would go back to his work as a news cameraman. And if the operation wasn't successful . . . oh, it didn't bear thinking about, and it might be all her fault. As Valerie Baker had so shrewdly pointed out, it would be a burden on her conscience for the rest of her life.

She drove back to the Inn, but she didn't tell Blythe where she had been or why. Somehow she got through the afternoon and at four o'clock went off to Isaac's house for a final rehearsal. Rose greeted her with an exclamation of concern.

'Lenore, what is the matter? You look so, how shall I put it? Strung-up? You are anxious about the concert, maybe?'

'A little.'

'But you shouldn't be. You play so well.'

'Not well enough for Isaac, though,' said Lenore, smiling at the violinist as he came out of the room where they usually rehearsed to welcome her.

'That is so, that is so,' he said, smiling back at her and taking hold of her arm affectionately to lead her into the room. 'But it is not the technique I criticise. That is perfect—no, brilliant. It is the lack of expression. You must learn to let go and let your feelings come through, and I have thought how I might help you in this. You must think of this trio as a little love story. The story of the ill-matched pair, the viola and the clarinet. Can you do that?'

'I'll try. But please tell me more,' said Lenore, intrigued by the suggestion.

'Listen, then.' Isaac picked up his viola and tucked it under his chin. 'While we wait for Jack we will talk, you and I, through our instruments, the ill-matched pair. As you know, the main theme of the first movement is stated first by me on the viola in a most quarrelsome fashion.' He played the tune in a vigorous way, and the sonorous sound of the instrument did suggest someone who was snarling irritably ... in the same way that Adam had snarled at her when they had first met, she thought. 'That is our hero, the viola, stating his position. He's a real tough guy ... what you call these days macho. Now you, on the clarinet, our heroine, play the same theme, but more ardently because you are female. Go on—play it now, with the feeling in mind that you like him and want to know more about him.'

Lenore, who had lifted her clarinet from its case and had put it together, wetted the reed with her lips, then began to play. The notes fell on the air clearly as pure as a bird's song as she remembered how she had felt when she had met Adam in his house, how she had tried to soften him. The memory grew, filled her mind, and the tone of the clarinet notes changed. They grew rounder and warmer, less disciplined, and when she came to the end of the tune and paused to take breath, Isaac clapped his hands in delight.

'That's it—that's it! Now I know that you have experience of what I'm saying. Now you do not play like a sexless being. Always, Lenore, you must bring your experience of life into your playing. So we move on to the second movement, that is lighthearted, although there are some serious moments, and in the trio section the clarinet sighs forth its yearning appeal, getting an immediate and exceedingly bad-tempered response from the viola. You begin to understand how it is like a love story. Advance and retreat, proposal and rejection.'

'Yes, I understand,' muttered Lenore. 'But how does it end . . . the love story, I mean?'

'In the last movement, as you know, the clarinet is given pride of place with two glorious melodies . . . the female expressing once and for all her love, and for a while the two ill-matched companions quarrel with each other as the viola—our hero—refuses to admit he has been conquered by love. Then at last, all opposition is overcome and viola and clarinet, our hero and heroine, go side by side in amity.'

'A happy ending?' asked Lenore.

'A happy ending. You will remember it while you play, please.'

'I'll try,' she whispered, then asked quickly, 'Isaac, you've been to Adam Jonson's house this week, haven't you?'

'A couple of times. To plan with Valerie Baker the arrangement of the room for the concert, the best views for the camera and that sort of thing. Also to make sure the chairs were delivered there from the church hall. Why do you ask?'

'Was Adam Jonson there? Did you see him?'

'The first time, yes. He had some advice to give us. But yesterday, no. He was not there, and Valerie was irritated because he had said he would be there. She asked Bertha Smith if he was at home, but the woman wouldn't tell her anything.'

'Do you know if he's going to be at the concert tomorrow?'

'No, I do not know that. But the Smiths will be there to open the house for us, and members of the Music and Arts Society will be on hand to direct people to their seats and to make sure no one wanders into the rest of the house. Ah, here is Jack, so we can get started. Now remember, Lenore, while you are playing you are a woman falling in love.'

It wasn't hard to remember, because she had fallen in love, and the music now seemed to tell the story of her affair with Adam right up to the middle of the last movement. Only the ending seemed beyond her reach, she thought sadly as she played the final few bars in unison with Isaac, because Adam had gone away and she would never see him again.

After the rehearsal both Isaac and Jack complimented her on the improvement in her playing, and they made arrangements to drive over to the Jonson house on the afternoon of the next day to make sure the room was ready and to have a final rehearsal. Jack drove her back to the Inn, where she found Blythe in the kitchen preparing to serve dinner to the few guests and Josh Kyd sitting at the table by the window, watching Blythe as she moved about, an expression of adoration in his grey eyes.

No happy ending for Blythe and him, either, Lenore thought as she went upstairs to her bedroom later. Oh, why was the path of true love never smooth? Why were there always obstacles in the way?

In bed, sleepless and watching the moon slide

from behind a cloud and shine directly through the bedroom window, she listened to the music of the Mozart trio beating through her mind, the viola gruff and growling, the clarinet plaintive and yearning. An ill-matched couple, Isaac had said, because musically speaking the instruments are so different from each other.

She and Adam were ill-matched. That was why they had clashed from the moment they had met. He was rough and tough and liked living dangerously, going to countries torn by warfare, taking films of violence. She was highly strung, sensitive to the nth degree, closing her eyes to and turning her back on the violence in the world, escaping from reality in the beauty of music. She and Adam had nothing in common. Nothing.

Then why this strong pull of attraction between them? Why was she in despair because he might die when undergoing an operation that he might not have had if she hadn't goaded him? Where was he now? In an impersonal hospital room, under sedation perhaps, sleeping in preparation for the operation tomorrow.

No. Tomorrow was a Sunday, and operations were rarely carried out on a Sunday. Only in the case of emergency. It would happen on Monday. Oh, God, if only she could find out when and where! No use asking Bertha Smith, but Albert might tell her. And once she knew she would go straight away to be there when the operation was done; to be there when Adam came out of the anaesthetic; to be there when—she forced herself to face up to the possibility again—when he died.

She slept that night better than she had slept any night since he had told her to stay away from him. It was as if, having admitted that she loved him in spite of his difference from her and having decided what to do once she knew where he was, her mind relaxed at last. She woke refreshed next morning, and while she was dressing she re-read Herzel's letter.

'Now that I've been apart from you for a while I realise how much I miss you. I should have asked you to come with me, I can see that now. I need you, Lenore. Will you fly out here and join me? We could live here together without my family knowing. Please come. . . .'

Lenore folded the letter up and pushed it back in the envelope, then stared out of the window at the morning sunlight slanting through the leaves of the trees. A bird was singing a repetitive tune. It seemed to her that it was *Too late, Herzel, too late, Herzel.* Opening the drawer in the table, she tossed Herzel's letter into it. One day she would reply to it, but not now. She had too much on her mind. She had Adam on her mind.

She tried to take it easy that day to keep her thoughts turned away from the concert. During the morning she helped Blythe prepare the usual Sunday brunch and also helped to wait on tables. Then she helped Blythe clear away dishes and when that was done she sat out in the garden to enjoy the sunshine. Later she changed into the simple navy blue and white crêpe-de-chine dress that she had chosen to wear for the concert, swept her hair up and pinned it in a knot on top of her head, made up her face and wearing her coat of thin grey ultra-suede, she carried her clarinet case downstairs and sat in the lounge until Isaac called for her. Blythe, who was catering the reception to be held at the house after the concert, would come later with Carrie, the regular waitress and, of course, Josh Kyd.

The late afternoon sunshine was golden, the distant hills were misty blue, the sea was a soft smooth violet, when Isaac's car approached the Jonson house. Albert Smith let them in. Neatly dressed in a navy blue suit and white shirt, he was almost unrecognisable as the person who had driven Lenore home early one morning more than a month ago.

Lenore let Isaac and Rose go ahead of her into the room where the concert would be held, and as soon as they were out of earshot she turned back to Albert, who was closing the front door.

'Is Adam ... I mean Mr Jonson ... all right?' she asked in a hoarse whisper.

Albert turned and looked down at her, his brow wrinkling in puzzlement.

'Sure he's all right, ma'am,' he drawled. 'Why shouldn't he be?'

'He ... well, someone told me he was going away to ... to hospital, and I wondered if he'd gone yet.'

Albert's twinkling blue eyes narrowed and he scratched the back of his head with a thumbnail.

'Now who would be telling you that?' he said—evasively, so Lenore thought.

'It doesn't matter who told me. Has he gone yet?'

'Well, he ain't here,' replied Albert.

'So where is he?' demanded Lenore with a touch of impatience.

'I dunno, ma'am. Are you playing in the concert tonight?'

'Yes, I am. Oh, Albert, please tell me where Adam is!'

'I'm not at liberty to do that, ma'am,' he replied stiffly. 'Adam wouldn't like it if I did. Now excuse me. I have to help Bertha set out the wine-glasses on trays.'

'Oh, damn,' muttered Lenore to his retreating back, and she stamped her foot on the floor, but he didn't look round or stop. He went right on along the passage to the kitchen.

Glancing to her left, she saw that the door of the room where she had slept with Adam was open. She went over and looked in. The room had changed. It was no longer furnished as a bedroom; it was a study, with a big carved desk, bookcases and comfortable chairs. Against one wall there was a long table covered with a white cloth. In the centre of the table was an arrangement of spring flowers; purple and yellow flags, pale narcissi and scarlet tulips. This would be where the reception took place, and it was no longer needed as a bedroom for Adam because he wasn't around any more. He'd gone. But where had he gone?

For the next couple of hours Lenore had no time to wonder about Adam's whereabouts and how she could find out where he was, because she was too busy with the last rehearsal before the concert and then having a quick sandwich dinner provided by Bertha. The concert was to start at seven-thirty, and at about six-thirty Jim Lorway and another cameraman arrived with their equipment. Valerie Baker wasn't with them.

'We don't know where she is,' explained Jim. 'I've been calling her apartment all day, but no answer. She hasn't been at the studios either. But I guess we can manage without her. We did before she ever came to the network, so we will again.'

She's with Adam, I know she is, thought Lenore, and felt a sickening surge of jealousy. *They've gone away together. They've gone back to New York. She's talked him out of having the operation and persuaded him to leave Northport. Oh, why am I wasting my time thinking about him? He made it very clear that he didn't want me once she came back into his life. Why don't I do what he told me to do? Forget him.*

At seven the audience began to arrive, sweeping up the driveway in all sizes and kinds of cars. Low in the western sky the sun lingered, a golden ball hovering above purple hills etched against duck-egg blue sky. The air was warm and soft, heady with the scent of lilacs and the tang of the sea. In the hallway of the old house the panelled walls glowed softly welcoming the strangers who had come, and soon the long wide room with the green velvet curtains and rosewood piano was full of the sound of voices.

'Is he here?' In the room that was now a study where the reception would be held Blythe was counting the wine-glasses that Bertha Smith had so carefully arranged on trays.

'Is who here?' asked Lenore, who had gone into the room to have a few words with her sister before the concert began.

'Adam Jonson, of course. I'd like to meet him.'

'No, he isn't. He's gone away. I think he's gone away with *her*.'

'Who?'

'Valerie Baker—you know, the producer of the programme. She was the woman you used to see in the village in the winter. She used to live here with Adam.'

'Really?' Blythe's dark eyes were round with surprise. Then she noticed the droop of Lenore's lips, the anguished look in the amber-coloured eyes. 'Too bad,' she commented. 'Too bad he isn't here—to hear you play, I mean. It was the least he could do.'

'I think so too,' muttered Lenore.

The concert started promptly. His face glowing rosily under the bright beams of the TV lamps, his short white summer jacket gleaming, Isaac introduced the Brahms quartet and then sat down to play. The sounds of two violins, a viola and a cello, sometimes strident and discordant, sometimes in beautiful harmony, sometimes in unison as they 'talked' together, filled the room. The audience sat still and silent. Outside the long windows shadows crept across the lawn as the sun set behind distant hills. Twilight lingered violet-grey, then darkness came. The only lights in the room were the blazing TV lights directed towards the musicians and the lights hanging above them. The rest of the room was in shadow.

The Brahms quartet ended triumphantly, every bow lifting off at the same time. There was a moment's silence and then the applause began. The four musicians bowed and then, carrying their instruments, walked out of the room through the open doorway into the hall. The clapping continued, so they walked back to take another bow.

'Are you ready?' Isaac asked Lenore, who had

been sitting in the hallway listening to the quartet and waiting for her turn.

'Yes, I am. But don't you and Jack want a drink or something before playing again?' she asked. 'You both look very hot.'

'It's the TV lights,' said Jack, mopping his face with a large white handkerchief. 'Even with the windows open it's hot in there.'

'I'm glad it's a fine night and we can have them open,' said Isaac. 'I think a little iced water would be good to drink.'

Blythe brought them glasses of water. They drank, settled their bow ties, made sure they had the right music and with Lenore leading the way returned to the room, where they were greeted with more applause.

The music began, and as the viola stated the main theme Lenore remembered what Isaac had told her the day before and imagined it was Adam snarling and swearing at her when she had collided with him on Bay Street. She raised her clarinet to her lips and the sound came out clear and rounded, repeating the same tune warmly, with emotion.

All through the first movement and again through the second she imagined she was arguing with and cajoling Adam; playing as if he were in the room. Then came the pause between the second and last movement, and she remembered what Isaac had said about the happy ending and wondered how she could make the music sound happy when she knew there was no hope of a happy ending for herself and Adam.

She looked into the shadowed audience, at the gleam of faces. Over heads she looked to the back of the room—and felt shock flicker through her. From the far back of the room her glance swerved sideways to one of the long open windows. A man was standing just inside the window. A tall man wearing dark glasses.

'Lenore, ready?' Isaac whispered, and she realised she had missed his signal to start playing. Collecting her wits about her, she nodded and lifted her clarinet. The reed pressed against her lower lip, and she blew softly. Adam was there by the window. He hadn't gone away. He was there listening to her. The notes came out rounded, golden, mellow.

Twice when she had a rest she glanced cautiously towards the window and stared for a moment at the shadowy figure, and was reassured that she wasn't imagining that he was there, yet when the music ended on its happy note of unison and the applause swelled and flowed around her, she looked again and he had gone.

The concert was an unqualified success, there was no doubt of that. Three times Lenore and the others had to take a bow, and afterwards in the reception they all received many handshakes and congratulations from the members of the audience who stayed for the reception. And all the time Lenore kept watching the doorway for Adam to appear. But he didn't come.

He must be somewhere in the house. If only she could leave the party and go in search of him! But she couldn't leave, not while Albert and Bertha were there making sure no one strayed upstairs or into the back of the house. She had to stay and drink wine and nibble at cheese and make polite conversation with people she didn't know.

It was after ten when the last member of the audience left and the musicians were able to leave too. Lenore declined the offer of a drive with Isaac, saying that she was going home with Blythe, but as she was going to get into Blythe's car she looked back at the house. Light still streamed out from the hallway through the open front door. It also glowed warm and yellow from a window on the second floor.

'Blythe, come here,' she whispered, and walked away from the car. Blythe followed her until they were out of earshot of Josh and Carrie, who were already in the car. 'Look,' Lenore pointed to the second-floor window. 'Adam is up there—I know he is. I saw him at the concert. He was standing by one of the windows. He's up there now, and I'm going to see him.'

'You want me to wait for you?' asked Blythe calmly.

'No, don't wait. You go home. But don't worry if I'm not back tonight, will you?'

'You're going to stay the night with him?'

'Yes, if . . . if it turns out that way I'm going to stay the night with him,' replied Lenore, and walking as quietly as she could, she went up the steps and into the house.

CHAPTER SEVEN

As soon as she stepped into the hallway Lenore heard voices, Bertha and Albert grumbling to one another as they came along the passage from the kitchen on their way to the front door. Quickly she stepped into the darkened room to the left, the study room, and stood behind the open door.

Voices and footsteps drew nearer. The light in the hallway was switched off. Someone closed the door of the study, and if it hadn't been for the moonlight trickling through the window she would have been engulfed in darkness. The front door was shut, then footsteps clumped down the steps. After a few minutes came the roar of Albert's truck starting up. The sound of it receded as it lumbered off down the driveway. In a few moments all was quiet.

Moving cautiously, Lenore groped her way to the door, found the knob, turned it and pulled open the door. The hallway was dark, but she soon found the light switch. Up the stairs she went, her heart thumping with excitement. She reached the dark upper hallway. Under a door on the right and at the front of the house was a thin line of yellow light. She went straight towards it, tapped lightly on the panels of the door and opened it without waiting to be invited in.

Light streamed across the wide bed, gleaming on the green and gold of the quilt. Adam was standing beside the bed with his back to her. He was dressed only in dark blue pyjama trousers and the skin of his broad back shone pale gold in the lamplight. He was turning down the bed covers and he seemed not to have heard her.

'Adam,' she said, and he stiffened all over, dropping the bedclothes, his head jerking back.

One crisp colourful oath and he swung around to face her. He was without his glasses and his slate-blue eyes were wide and staring at something over her head.

'God, are you here again?' he snarled. 'I thought I told you to stay away from me!'

'Yes, you did. And I did stay away . . . but when I heard that you're going away soon to hospital I had to come and see you again. I had to,' she whispered—and suddenly it happened. The love she felt for him burst out and flowed through her and she let it flow out of her, warm and strong, as resistless as the tide coming from the deep places of the sea, urging her towards him, her hands outstretched, reaching out to touch him.

In three strides she was close to him, her hands on his chest sliding up over the scarred skin to his shoulders, lifting to the nape of his neck.

'Oh, Adam, I was so glad when I saw you standing by the window at the concert,' she whispered. 'I thought you'd gone away, you see. I thought we'd never meet again.' Overcome by her emotions, she pressed her lips against the pulsing hollow at the base of his throat and licked his salty skin.

He stayed stiff and still in her embrace for only a moment. Then with a sound that was half groan, half sigh, he dropped his defences.

Roughly his hands curved about her face and lifted it. She had a brief glimpse of his half-blind eyes, burning blue, his hard lips softening sensually, and then his mouth was on hers, hot and demanding, and the white-heat of passion was flaming up again, melding them together.

Somehow her coat was taken from her and tossed to the floor. Across the bed they fell together, still kissing mouth to mouth, greedily. Under Adam's frantic fingers her dress came apart, and then his lips were searing the soft white swell of her breast and she was twisting and groaning in an agony of desire, her nails scratching his skin.

Quick and fiery was their coming together, born of their desperate desire, violent and yet triumphant. As from a great distance Lenore heard herself crying out, heard Adam's gasps and groans. Everything swung around her crazily, they seemed to flow into each other, and fulfilment was a sweet, slow weakness and the only sound was the quick beating of their hearts in unison.

Her mind was still spinning when he withdrew from her sharply, hurting her, as if in repudiation of what they had just enjoyed together. Missing his warmth and weight, aware that something was wrong, Lenore opened her eyes. Adam was sitting on the edge of the bed and his head was between his hands. She sat up, curling her legs beneath her, and touched his shoulder, lightly trailing her fingers over his warm slightly moist skin.

'Adam, what's wrong?' she whispered.

'You ought not to have come here,' he

muttered. 'I told you to stay away from me. You ought not to have come. You must have guessed what would happen if you came here alone.'

There was a short tense silence, while Lenore stared at the proud leonine head that was turned away from her, at the broad shoulders, and tried to probe the enigma of him. Failing, she whispered,

'I wanted it to happen. I'm glad it happened, and I want it to happen again. Tonight. Only . . .' she paused as laughter shook her voice, 'only perhaps a little more slowly next time,' she continued softly. '*Lente* and *pianissimo* before moving into a *crescendo* that will take us to a wonderful, beautiful climax!'

His hand dropped away from his head and he turned sharply towards her, frowning.

'What the hell are you talking about?' he rasped.

'About making love,' she murmured. 'I came here to make love to you tonight before . . . before you go away.'

'Who told you I'm going away?' he demanded. 'Albert?'

'No—Valerie Baker. She said you'd decided to have an operation to remove the pressure that's causing your blindness. She said there's only a sixty–forty chance of its being successful.' Her voice began to shake with the intensity of her emotions. He was looking at her, right at her as if he could see her, and his face was set in hard cynical lines. Slowly she reached out a hand and laid it on his forearm. Golden hairs were silky beneath her fingers and the muscle tensed, but he didn't shake her hand off. 'Was . . . was Valerie right, Adam?' she whispered.

'She was right,' he replied, his frown deepening. 'Though why the hell she told you I can't figure out.'

'She told me because she wanted me to believe it would be my fault if . . . if you die when you're having the operation. She said you'd only decided to go through with it because someone . . . and she had guessed it was me . . . had accused you of not being normal while you're half blind,' she said in a low shaken voice. 'Oh, Adam, is it true? Did you tell her I'd said that to you?'

'The bitch, the damned interfering bitch!' he snarled, and covered her hand with his, long fingers gripping painfully. 'Yes, I did tell her. We were having an argument and she . . . oh, hell, to understand you'd have to know about her and me. . . .' He broke off, swearing softly under his breath, half turning away from her.

'Then tell me,' Lenore urged quietly. 'I . . . I know she's been your mistress.'

His head jerked around. The slate blue eyes had widened incredulously.

'She has?' he asked mockingly. 'This is news to me. When?'

'When . . . when you returned to New York after assignments abroad. When she came here to live here with you before last Christmas,' she said uncertainly.

'And you believed her. You dared to believe her!' His voice purred threateningly as he leaned towards her, his hand still grasping hers where it lay on his arm, his bulky shoulders looming as he pushed her backwards against the pillows. 'Once and once only, long ago, so long ago that I've forgotten it, when we were still students at college, I spent a night with Valerie.' His lips drew back over his teeth. 'It was a mistake,' he hissed, 'one which she's made me regret time and time again. You see, she's one of the possessive kind. I'd made love to her once and then had left her, and that she could never forgive, so ever since she's turned up in my life and tried to take possession whenever she could. She thought she'd got me when I came here, half blind and nearly out of my mind with pain and frustration. She was going to be my helpmate, my guide through the semi-darkness that surrounded me, my guardian angel.' His laugh was short and mirthless. 'Anyone less suited to the part it would be hard to find! What she really wanted was to dominate me. She was also after the money I'd just inherited. It didn't take me long to figure out what she was doing. She gave herself away by urging me not to have the operation when she heard about it. "Don't have it, Adam, you might die. You don't need to have it when you have me to help you. I'll be your guide, your helper, if you'll marry me".' His laugh crackled with unkind mockery. 'Thank God Albert was here! He helped me to get rid of her, had her bags packed and ready at the door when I told her to get out. He drove her away in his truck too, out of my life—for ever, I hoped.' His lips twitched with bitter humour. 'I was wrong again.'

'You didn't know she'd got a job with the local public TV network then?'

'No. I'd never have agreed to let them film the concert here if I'd known she'd be involved. I was furious when she turned up, so furious I lashed out at you, told you to stay away from me.' He drew his hand across his throat. 'I'd had it up to here with pushy interfering women!'

'Oh. You ... you think I'm pushy?' Lenore's eyes began to sparkle dangerously.

'A bit,' he taunted softly, leaning closer. 'You wouldn't be here now on my bed if you weren't.' Bending his head, he nibbled the lobe of her right ear tantalisingly.

Her hands on his shoulders, she tried to hold him off.

'If you think that of me ... I'm not staying with you a minute longer,' she gasped breathlessly. 'Oh, please let me go, Adam. Please!'

His mouth smothered her plea and at once her struggles to escape from him, because this kiss was different. It was sweet and reverent and she succumbed readily to its seduction, parting her lips and letting them quiver against his in a delicate mothlike response.

Sliding off her so that he lay on his side, Adam turned her towards him, caressing her back with long strokes of his hands, and slowly, softly it began, the build-up of the exquisite sensations as they both explored tenderly the secret parts of each other's body, worshipping with hands and lips and tongues.

'I wish I could see you properly. I wish I could see you,' Adam groaned when passion began to throb uncontrollably through both of them, surging through their loins.

'You will one day,' Lenore whispered breathlessly, framing his face and kissing his eyes.

He didn't say anything, but overwhelmed her suddenly, taking her possessively and coaxing her to rise with him to a swelling, glorious climax, and afterwards they lay silent for a while, at peace with each other, knowing they would always be a part of each other no matter what came between them in the future.

And something would come between them to separate them. Soon. The thought crept unbidden into Lenore's mind, chilling her.

'Adam?'

'Mmm?' He sounded half asleep. His head was resting against her shoulder, his arm was about her waist and one sinewy leg was sprawled across both of hers.

'When ... when did you decide to go for the operation?'

'I'm not sure. Why do you want to know?' His speech was slurred, indifferent. He sounded as if he didn't want to talk.

'Was it before or after I said what I did about ... about you not being normal?'

He was silent for a few moments. Then he moved away from her and rolled on to his back. Reaching out, he switched off the bedside lamp. The room was plunged into darkness which was only slightly relieved by faint moonlight.

'Before,' he said clearly and firmly. 'My decision had nothing to do with anything you said and was the result of long and painful arguments with myself. I decided in the end that it's my life and I'd rather die than live on, half blind, unable to do the things I want to do. That's the chance I'm taking by having the operation. Dangerously is the only way I know how to live.'

Lenore's turn to be silent as she fought to contain the tears that sprang to her eyes.

'I'm glad,' she said when she felt she was under control and was able to speak coolly. 'I'm glad your decision had nothing to do with what I said. I wouldn't be able to bear it if . . . if you died and it was my fault.' Her voice broke on the last word.

He moved immediately, looming over her, a dark shape in the darkness. His fingers trailed lightly across her cheeks, tracing the course of teardrops that had spilled. He came closer to her, the warmth and scents of his body were all around her making her head spin. His tongue licked the tears from her lashes and he spoke softly.

'Lenore, you mustn't weep for me. I'm not worth it.'

'But you are, you are!' she cried out, flinging her arms around his neck, trapping him against her.

'You don't know what you're saying. You don't know what I'm like—really like, I mean,' he said gruffly, rubbing his nose against her.

'I've got a good idea,' she retorted. 'You're rough and tough, cynical and hard—and chauvinistic into the bargain. You're not at all the sort of man I *like* . . . but I *love* you just the same.'

'Stop romanticising me,' he growled.

'And I don't want you to die,' she went on wildly as if he had never spoken.

He stiffened, reared up and taking hold of her wrists pulled her hands away from his neck.

'You're not going to ask me not to have that operation just for your sake, I hope,' he said sneeringly.

'No, I'm not, but I don't want you to die. I

want you to live. When? When are you leaving to go to the hospital?'

'Tomorrow—in the morning. Albert is going to drive me down to the clinic,' Adam seemed to realise he was still holding her wrists. His grip tightened on them rather cruelly and twisting on to his back again he pulled her roughly down on top of him. 'We haven't much time left,' he said huskily, 'so how about you showing me how much you love me before I go?'

The moon had set and dawn was paling the eastern sky before they slept, sinking into the sodden oblivion of satiation and exhaustion. So deeply did she descend into slumber, Lenore did not hear the rap of Albert Smith's knuckles on the door of the bedroom or his calling of Adam's name. Nor did she hear Adam answer. She was unaware of his stealthy movements as he rolled out of the bed and dressed. She did not feel either his kiss on her cheek, the tender touch of his fingers at her temple, and she did not hear the door open and close when he left the room.

When she did open her eyes and saw the sunlight laying a path of yellow light across the floor she knew immediately where she was and what had happened, yet still she turned her head hopefully to where Adam had lain beside her, hoping to see the ruffled golden hair, the broad, lined brow, the wide-set slate blue eyes, the straight blunt-ended nose, the bitter-sweet curve of his mouth.

But he had gone, and she couldn't be sure she would ever see him again, for if he lived and regained his sight he would never come back to

Northport and he would never look for her. He had made that very plain several times during the night, warning her in subtle ways.

'No matter what happens, sweetheart, we've always had this together,' he had whispered.

Remembered rapture, that was all she would have of him, and nothing more. Closing her eyes, she let the memories of the night crowd into her mind, but they hurt too much, so she opened her eyes again quickly and flinging off the bedclothes, swung out of bed and began to dress. She must leave immediately, before Bertha arrived and found her in Adam's bed.

If she had accepted his proposal when he had made it they might have been married by now, she thought as she wandered down the driveway under the feathery branches of the sighing pines. They might have been married and she would have had the right to go with him to the hospital, to have waited there during the operation, to have been there when he had come round.

But he wouldn't have liked that, she realised now. He didn't want to be possessed. Then why had he asked her to marry him? She had put the question to him in the night and he had answered evasively, she had thought,

'I've told you why—I wasn't behaving normally. Maybe I was testing you to find out how far you were prepared to go to get what you wanted. Maybe I suspected you were after my money like Valerie,' he had taunted her.

'Then you must have been very relieved when I refused,' she had retorted tartly.

'Oh, I was. Very,' he had replied, mockery edging his voice, and had prevented her from retaliating by kissing her, and when he was kissing her she ceased to be reasonable and intelligent and became instead wild and wanton, a mass of tingling desire.

Strong, masterful, in spite of his disability, Adam had gone, and yet he was still with her, filling her mind, leaving no room for anyone else, and while she stayed in Northport where they had first met it would always be like that. But she wasn't going away. Not yet. She had to stay a little longer, at least until she knew whether he had survived the operation or not. She had to stay, because the Smiths were her only contact with him. Albert, as Adam's only surviving next of kin, would be the first to be informed of the result of the operation.

Lenore reached the end of Pickering Lane and turned into Main Street. High above the elm trees were in leaf, tufts of tender green waving lightly in the wind. The long shadows of the trunks slanted across the road and sunlight glinted on the windows of old houses. At the Inn the lilac bushes were in full bloom, delicate pale purple and creamy blossoms nodding, wafting their heady scent about.

Going in by the back door, Lenore found Blythe there sitting with Josh Kyd at the table. They had been drinking coffee and were holding hands, but when they saw her they withdrew their hands from the table and looked a little shy and self-conscious. Josh stood up.

'Guess it's time I went back to work,' he decided. He paused and gave Lenore a shy glance. 'That was a good concert last night—I enjoyed it. I hope you're going to stay on in Northport and play some more for us.'

'Why, thank you,' said Lenore, surprised by the compliment. He'd never really spoken directly to her before and there had been times when she had felt he resented her presence in the Inn because she distracted Blythe's attention away from him.

'See you later,' he added with a sidelong glance at Blythe, and strode to the door.

When the door had closed behind him, Lenore looked at her sister. It seemed to her that Blythe looked beautiful that morning. Her hair shone like a blackbird's wing, her dark eyes glowed with a mysterious light and her cheeks were delicately flushed.

'Something's happened,' said Lenore. 'Between you and Josh.'

'Yes, it has.' Blythe smiled dreamily. 'He's asked me to marry him.'

'But what about. . . .'

'He's heard from his lawyer. He can get a divorce now on the grounds of desertion by his wife. For three years she's refused to come and live here with him and has made no attempt to see him. He came to tell me straight away and then asked me to marry him when the divorce is final.'

'And you—what do you want? Do you want to marry him?'

'Of course I do! I want to be married, to have children before I get much older and I want Josh to be their father. Oh, Lenore, I'm so happy! I never thought it would happen to me. I thought I'd always be single because I couldn't marry Josh.'

'And I'm happy too, for you,' whispered

Lenore, hugging her sister, the quick tears filling her eyes as her vulnerable emotions were touched.

'Have you had any breakfast?' asked Blythe when the hug was over.

'No.'

'Then sit down and I'll cook you some,' said Blythe practically. She poured coffee from the pot into a mug. 'Here, take this and go and sit down, and while I'm cooking tell me about Adam Jonson. Did you see him?'

'Yes.'

'And?'

'I stayed the night with him,' said Lenore flatly.

Blythe gave her a worried sidelong glance, then turned her attention again to the eggs she was beating for an omelette.

'I hope you know what you're doing,' she sighed.

'It's all right, Blythe. He's gone, and the chances of my ever having anything to do with him any more are very remote.' Lenore forced herself to speak quietly and coolly. 'He's having an operation to remove the pressure that's making him blind. It's one of those touchy jobs. He ... he could die.' Her voice faltered. She stopped and took a gulp of coffee. It scalded her throat.

'And if he doesn't die? If the operation is a success and he can see properly again?' asked Blythe, maintaining her disapproving manner.

'He'll go back to being a news cameraman, I guess, and to living dangerously,' replied Lenore tonelessly, looking out at the garden, pretending an indifference to what the future held for Adam that she didn't feel. All the trees at the bottom of the garden were either in leaf or foaming with blossom now, the deep rich green of maples contrasting with the delicate silver-green of birches and the dark red of ornamental crab-apples. 'Has the mail come yet?' she asked casually, more to change the course of conversation than from any real interest.

'Yes. But there was nothing for you,' said Blythe, pouring egg batter into hot melted butter. 'By the way, Isaac called. He wants to see you as soon as possible. He's upset about that Baker woman. It seems she quit the TV network without warning—just walked out, and now there's a possibility that the programme of concerts won't go on because she isn't there to edit the films. I wonder why she left?'

'I don't know,' said Lenore. She wasn't going to say anything about Valerie because that would bring Adam into the conversation again, and from now on discussion with Blythe or anyone else about Adam was taboo, strictly prohibited, because discussing him seemed somehow to desecrate what they had known together, those few hours of passionate love, the rapture that had been theirs and that no one could take away from them. Star-crossed, ill-matched she and Adam might be, but they had for a short time discovered the essence of each other and had shared a private beautiful world of their own creating. 'I'll go and see Isaac as soon as I've eaten,' she went on. 'I'm sure Jim Lorway could produce the programme and I'll be more than willing to help him with the editing.'

True to her word, she walked round to Isaac's house later and as a result of her conversation with him drove to Bangor with him that afternoon to see the programme manager of the TV network and discuss with him what could be done about continuing to film the series of concerts. When they left soon after four o'clock, Lenore had a job for the rest of the summer, to produce and co-edit with Jim Lorway.

'I bet Isaac is ecstatic,' remarked Blythe when Lenore told her the news.

'Yes, he is,' said Lenore, laughing a little. 'All the way back from Bangor he kept clapping his hands together and saying, "It's wonderful. I'm so happy—happy for you, happy for me." I had to grab the steering wheel several times to keep the car on the right side of the road. These people who talk with their hands make dangerous drivers!'

'I'm happy for you and happy for me too,' said Blythe. 'Happy that you'll be staying here for the rest of the summer and happy that you'll have something to do to . . . well, to keep your mind busy and off a certain person. How do you feel about the job?'

'Bewildered,' sighed Lenore. 'But excited too. It will be a challenge, one I never expected. The experience will certainly be valuable, and if I'm any good at producing it will broaden my options when it comes to looking for jobs in the future. But I'm still hoping to be taken on by the orchestra in Caracas.'

'When are you going to put on the next concert? People have already been asking me if there are to be more.'

'About the first of July. Mother will be here then, won't she?'

'I'm not sure now. Last time I talked to her on the phone she said something about going over to Scotland instead. Apparently there's going to be a family reunion of all the Frazers and her Scottish cousins have invited her to be there in July. Will you have the concert in the same place?'

'We're hoping to,' replied Lenore coolly. 'That was the arrangement Isaac made with Adam Jonson and there's no reason to believe it's been changed, but Isaac and I will be going over to the house later this week to talk to Albert Smith about it. I guess Adam has left him in charge.'

'When you were at the TV studios in Bangor, was anything said about Valerie Baker?' asked Blythe curiously.

'Very little. I got the impression that she wasn't very popular and that they were glad she'd quit. They'd been looking for ways of firing her.'

'Didn't she give a reason for quitting?'

'Only that she wanted to return to New York because she found Maine too slow and un-stimulating,' said Lenore. 'Do you want me to help you this evening?'

'No, thanks. Carrie is here and we don't have many bookings for dinner.'

'Then I think I'll answer some letters,' said Lenore, starting up the stairs.

'Herzel's letter?' queried Blythe with a wicked glint.

'Perhaps,' retorted Lenore, and went on up to her room.

Three days slipped by; days of mixed weather, sunshine and showers alternating; days of anxious waiting for Lenore, waiting for news of Adam, waiting to go to his house where she would see Albert Smith and could ask him whether the operation had been done or not, and if it had been done whether it had been successful or not.

But to her great disappointment Albert wasn't at the house on Pickering Point when she and Isaac arrived. Only Bertha was there, opening the door and letting them into the house reluctantly, staring at them with her large grey watery eyes, her small mouth pursed up primly.

'Albert ain't back yet from Boston,' she said in her abrupt way. 'And I dunno nothing about you using that room again. If I had my way you wouldn't have it. A rare mess I had to clean up after the last time!'

Her remarks devastated Isaac and he apologised profusely over and over again, until Lenore, who had the measure of the forthright, unco-operative Bertha by now, cut in with,

'When will Albert come back?'

'Next Monday, he says. Depends.'

'On what?' demanded Lenore.

'On how Adam is feeling.'

'Oh, has Mr Jonson been ill? I didn't know,' said Isaac.

'Not ill—just operated on,' said Bertha. 'His head, to make him see.

'Has the operation been done?' asked Lenore.

'Sure has—day before yesterday. But they don't know the results yet. That's why Albert's still there. Blood's thicker than water, so they say, and Albert sure is thick with Adam. Treats him as if he was his son instead of his cousin a few times removed,' said Bertha, and moved towards the front door to open it. 'Reckon you won't be staying, since Albert isn't here, so I'll show you out.'

About to step outside, Lenore turned back to glance appealingly at Bertha.

'Please would you ask Albert to phone me when he comes back?' she asked.

'You'll have to leave your number,' replied Bertha grudgingly. 'Hang on and I'll get you a paper and pen.'

She went into the study room and returned with a small pad of paper. Lenore wrote her name and the telephone number of the Inn on it and a few words for Albert: *Please let me know about Adam*. Then after thanking Bertha she followed Isaac down the steps and to his car.

They made the return trip to Northport in unusual silence—unusual, because usually Isaac chattered all the time. Three more days before she would have more news of Adam, thought Lenore. Three more days of anxiety and prayer. Not that she was a praying person; she didn't go into a church and get down on her knees and bow her head every day. Nor did she kneel by her bedside every night. But she thought of Adam constantly and hoped fervently that the operation had been a success and he would see properly again, even though the restoration of his sight would mean that he would go away from her. And that was a sort of praying, she maintained.

Saturday, Sunday and Monday. The three days dragged in spite of the business of the weekend when there were more guests staying at the Inn than ever before and she and Blythe and Carrie were rushed off their feet, cooking, waiting on tables and clearing up afterwards. Monday was the worst, and when the day ended without any call from Albert Lenore spent the night wondering if he had been delayed because the results of the operation had been negative; perhaps because Adam . . . had died.

She was practising on her clarinet the next morning, trying to immerse herself completely in the art of making music in an effort to forget her anxiety about Adam, when Carrie came up to tell her that Albert Smith was in the lounge and wanted to see her.

Long and lean in his overalls, he was studying an oil painting of a fishing schooner that was hanging on one of the walls of the lounge, and when she entered breathless from having run down the stairs he cocked a bright blue eye at her, pointed to the painting and said,

'The *Mary Day*—she's still sailing. I seen her in Camden when I came through there yesterday. She's one of them cruise schooners now, sails about the islands with a lot of landlubbers on board. Food's good, they say.' He gave her another glance. 'Got yer note,' he added. 'Didn't phone 'cos I don't like talking on the phone, so I came over this morning.'

'Thank you. Won't you sit down? Can I get you something? A cup of coffee?' asked Lenore, her voice quivering as she tried to contain her impatience.

'No, thanks. I'll just say what I have to say and be on my way. Adam had the operation.'

'Yes. And?'

'He came through pretty well, didn't die or anything like that. But he's low.'

'Low?' queried Lenore in bewilderment.

'Depressed. That's why I stayed on a bit. He hoped he'd be able to see right away, as soon as he'd recovered from the anaesthetic. But it weren't that way at all, so he was mad. You know the way he gets when things don't go his way, snarling at the surgeon, the nurses, me, everyone who went near him.'

'I know,' murmured Lenore. 'But will he see?'

'Won't know for about six weeks to two months.'

'That's a long time to wait. For him, I mean.'

'You're darned right it is! He's likely to go crazy,' drawled Albert, seeming to relish the fact of Adam going mad and behaving badly as a result. 'Wouldn't like to be the nurses who are going to be looking after him.'

'Oh, he isn't coming back here, then?' she asked.

'Nope. Going to stay in a special convalescent place outside New York.'

'Oh, I didn't know.' Lenore thought suddenly of Valerie Baker, who had returned to New York because she found Maine dull and unstimulating. Or was it because she had known Adam was going to the big city? 'Albert, do you think I could visit him, at the convalescent home?' she asked urgently.

'You could, I guess,' he drawled, chewing for a few seconds while he considered her with shrewd blue eyes, 'but if you take my advice, you won't go near him.'

'Oh, why not?'

'Adam don't like being chased by women.'

'But I wouldn't be chasing him,' she retorted. 'I'd be going as a friend . . . to cheer him up.'

'He won't like it.' He chewed some more, then said, 'You want for him to treat you like he treated that sassy New York woman?'

'You mean Valerie Baker?'

'That's her. Came to see him the day after the operation. I told her to get lost. Adam wouldn't have liked for her to have seen him with all those tubes and things stuck up his nose and into his arm. She's got no respect for a man's privacy, that one. But she's persistent, I give her that. Came again, with a bouquet of flowers, when I wasn't there to shoo her off.'

'What happened?' asked Lenore.

'Adam got so mad he shouted and roared, and the nurses had to ask her to leave.' Albert loped towards the door leading into the hallway. 'Guess it's time I was on my way,' he announced.

Lenore followed him to the front door of the Inn. As he opened it he glanced down at her.

'If you do go to see Adam don't take him no flowers. He'll only throw them right back at you, and that's a waste of good flowers. Be seein' ya!'

CHAPTER EIGHT

LENORE took Albert's advice and didn't go to visit Adam, because Albert was right and she didn't want Adam to treat her as he had treated Valerie Baker. Also, she didn't want Adam to think she was chasing him. In fact the more she thought about it the more she realised the wisdom of staying away from him while he was convalescing. If he wanted her, if he loved her, he would come to her one day. Meanwhile her life had to go on without him as it had before she had met him. There were things she wanted to do that had nothing to do with him, just as he had things he wanted to do that had nothing to do with her. They didn't have to live in one another's pockets all the time just because they had shared a few hours of passion. They were adults, not adolescents.

But she ached for him—oh, how she ached and hurt, deep down. And she longed to know how he was, how he looked, how he was feeling. She tried to write to him, but the thought of some nurse having to read the letter to him if he couldn't see to read it stopped her, and in the end she sent him only a note, one of those letter notes that you can buy in a packet at a novelty store, with prints of local scenes or paintings of flowers on them. Inside she wrote simply,

'Adam, Thinking of you always, Lenore.'

The next time she saw Albert she asked him

for the address of the convalescent home where
Adam was staying, and when he heard that she
didn't intend to go and see Adam, he gave it to
her.

'Have you heard how he is?' she asked.

'He's pretty good,' Albert said laconically,
chewing rhythmically, looking over her head at
something she couldn't see.

'Can he see properly yet?'

'Nope.'

'How much longer will he be there?'

'No saying.'

And making his usual excuse that it was time
he was on his way, Albert strode away from her.

The days of June passed by, sometimes
gloriously sunny, with the water in the estuary
blue and sparkling, sometimes shrouded in thick
down-east fog, grey and wet, always shifting and
swirling, blotting out view of hills and islands.
Life in Northport followed its usual routine. At
Josh Kyd's boatyard sailing yachts were launched
and swung at their moorings in the estuary
awaiting the arrival of their owners who would
come when most summer vacations began on July
the first. Guests, mostly elderly or childless
couples taking their vacations before the annual
rush of families from New York and Boston to
the coast, arrived at the Inn. They stayed a few
days or a week exploring the local countryside
and the many small seaports, then moved on.

The music group met regularly and rehearsed
for the next concert, which was planned for the
first of July and not the middle of the month as
had been arranged originally. The first concert
had attracted new members, both amateur and

professional performers, including several wind instrumentalists.

'Now we can extend our repertoire,' announced Isaac enthusiastically. 'We can at last perform some of Mozart's divertimenti. I propose for the next concert we play the Divertimento in B flat for two clarinets, two bassoons and two horns, to be followed by Beethoven's Trio No. 6 in B flat for piano, violin and cello. It will make a good evening, you'll see.'

Having to practise and rehearse for the Divertimento as well as having to help produce the programme for TV made Lenore extremely busy. But she enjoyed the involvement with so many new acquaintances, and of course there was always the great and serene pleasure of performing Mozart's beautiful music. Jim Lorway was easy to work with and fell in with her suggestions about where the cameras should be placed during the concert. She learned that in the production of a film timing was all-important and had to plan with Jim at rehearsals when the camera should zoom in on a particular performer.

After seeing the films of Valerie's interviews with herself and Isaac, Jack, Willa and Jane, she and Jim decided to scrap them and to start all over again. Jim persuaded her to do the interviewing of the other musicians herself.

'It's better for you to ask the questions because you know so much about the music as well as what it's like to be a performer,' he said. 'And then you have a good presence on film. You photograph well and you convey a sincerity that Valerie lacked.' He grinned at her. 'It's those big golden eyes,' he mocked.

'Really?' exclaimed Lenore, amazed by this view of herself.

'Sure. You're natural and spontaneous. You don't hold anything back or hide your feelings, and you come over on film as someone who's warm and genuinely interested in and excited by what you're doing. And that's what TV viewers like. They can soon spot a phoney. That's why Valerie didn't have much success as an interviewer. She was too wrapped up in herself, in the projection of her own image on the screen, and not interested enough in the people she was interviewing. She wasn't all that good as a producer either. Not enough imagination and not enough respect for the intelligence of the people out there watching the TV. I'm not surprised she's never been able to hold a job down with a network.'

The second concert was even more of a success than the first. It was attended not only by local people but also by many summer residents of the area, and tourists. Every seat was sold and many people had to stand or sit on the stairs in the hallway. It received good reviews in the local press.

Afterwards the music group met as usual to evaluate the concert and to plan the next one. Once again the suggestion was made that on the strength of the success of the concerts Northport ought to have its own music and arts festival every summer.

'The town council is interested because it will attract more summer visitors and tourists to the area,' said Fred Caplan, who was a member of the council. 'If we could only be sure of getting the Jonson house.' He gave Lenore a glance. 'Did you ever mention the idea of a festival to Adam Jonson?'

'No, I didn't. At the time I thought it was enough that he agreed to let us use the big room for this summer's concerts,' she replied cautiously.

'Anyone else bring up the matter with him?' asked Fred, looking round the group. 'What about you, Isaac? You seemed to click with Jonson.'

'Yes, I talked about a festival,' replied Isaac. 'But I didn't push it too much. Like Lenore, I thought we ought to step carefully, wait and see how the concerts went over before doing anything else.'

'Well, they're going over great,' said Jack. 'And I think we ought to approach Jonson now as a group. We could write a letter to him setting out exactly what it is we want to do and send it to him. I think Lenore knows where he is, don't you?' He turned to her enquiringly.

'I can find out,' she said. 'I'll ask Albert Smith—he'll know.'

She made a point of going to see Albert the next day. As usual he wasn't very communicative, but he told her that Adam was still unable to see properly and that he was still at the rehabilitation clinic outside New York.

After much discussion the music group composed a letter and it was signed by Isaac and Jack and sent to Adam, then all their energies were applied to the planning of the third concert for the first week in August and the fourth concert at the end of August, just before all the summer visitors departed.

Lenore at last received a letter from the hiring committee of the orchestra in Caracas to say she had not been appointed to play in the woodwind section after all. With disappointment at being rejected came a certain relief. At last she knew where she stood and could start making other plans for her future. She told Isaac what had happened and asked if she could use his name as a reference when she applied for other auditions with other orchestras.

'Sure you can use my name,' he said. 'I'll be delighted to give you a letter of reference. But couldn't you stay here? The group needs you, Lenore, and if we can only get going on this music festival we would very much like you to be the executive director of it.'

'I'd like to stay. And I'd like to direct the festival. But I have to eat,' she replied. 'I can't sponge for ever on Blythe.'

'I understand. But you still have the small job of producing the next two concerts for TV, and I have this feeling the network might want you to do more. Why not wait and see what September brings, my dear? Much can happen between then and now.'

'I guess so,' agreed Lenore with a sigh. 'Has there been any reply to the letter you sent to Adam Jonson?'

'No, not yet. But it will come. It will come,' he said. 'He will not ignore us—I'm sure of that.'

The third concert was performed and rehearsals started for the fourth one. The hot days of August passed by, golden and blue, sometimes bright and windy, with the bay and the estuary dotted with the sails of many yachts; sometimes still and heavy, deteriorating into violent thunder-storms with tropical-style rainstorms and brilliant displays of lightning.

The last day of the month, a Sunday, was perfect. The sunset was spectacular, the sky flushed with crimson light and the sea looking as if it had been set on fire. The hills were darkest purple.

At the Jonson house the sound of music, classical, modern and contemporary, flowed out from the open windows of the long wide room. The audience sat entranced. And Lenore, who was not performing that night but was intro-ducing each piece before it was played and so was seated behind the piano where she couldn't be seen by the audience, was sure that the spirit of Martin Jonson must have been smiling and nodding in approval of what was happening in the room where he had so often played the piano.

It was when she was ending her introduction to the final piece of music and was standing in front of the piano that she saw Adam. At least, she thought she saw him. The sight of him jarred her so much that she stopped speaking in the middle of a sentence and had to take a deep breath before going on.

Before she went back to her seat behind the piano she glanced quickly again at the open window where she thought she had seen him standing. But he wasn't there, and she was convinced then that her imagination was playing tricks on her. She wanted so much to see him that perhaps her mind had flipped and she had begun to hallucinate.

The concert ended. The audience applauded.

The performers made several bows. Slowly the chattering excited crowd left the house to drive away in cars or to walk through the soft starlit darkness.

After arranging to meet at Isaac's house during the next week the performers also left. Lenore said goodnight to Jim Lorway and the other cameraman and they went off in their van. She had come alone in Blythe's car, and as she opened the door on the driver's side she looked hopefully back at the dark bulk of the house, remembering the night of the first concert and the light shining out from an upstairs window.

But there was no light upstairs and no light downstairs either, yet she could see the front door was still open. She looked around. Albert Smith's truck had gone, and there was only one other car parked in front of the house, far away from hers. She could just make out the gleam of its hub-caps and windows.

She slammed the door of the car shut and hurried up the front steps and into the hallway. Darkness surged around her. She stepped into the music room. Faint light trickling in through the windows glinted on the piano keys, on the rows of chairs, on the clock on the marble shelf above the fireplace. At the open windows the velvet curtains stirred in the evening breeze.

A sound from the hallway made her whirl round. She looked out of the music room. The front door was closed. Still in darkness, she went towards it, turned the knob and pulled. The door was locked. Albert must have been in the house and now he had left, locking the door after him. The back door was probably locked too. She was locked in the house.

No, she wasn't. The windows in the music room were still open—careless of Albert to forget them. Lenore went back into the room and began to edge around the rows of chairs in the direction of the nearest window. Behind her someone called her name.

'Lenore!'

She half turned towards the doorway of the room. She couldn't see anyone. Was she imagining the voice? Had someone spoken her name? Or was this room haunted?

'Lenore.' Soft yet hollow, the voice spoke again. Goosebumps prickled her skin. Fear of the unknown took over and she began to hurry towards the window, walking into chairs and pushing them away from her violently so that they crashed noisily into each other. She reached the window and was going to step outside when from behind her a well-known, longed-for voice roared,

'Lenore, what the hell are you doing here?'

Her skin clammy with sweat, her heart thudding against her ribs, her eyes wide with terror, she glanced back. Light flooded the room. A man was standing just inside the door, his right hand dropping away from the switch on the wall. A man she knew yet didn't know. A big tough-looking man, looking even tougher because his hair was very short, looking as if it was growing again after it had been shaved off. He was dressed in jeans and a short-sleeved blue T-shirt. The thin material clung to his muscular chest and the short sleeves showed off his tanned sinewy arms. He wasn't wearing dark glasses and across the room Lenore could see the blue sparkle of his eyes.

'Adam,' she whispered, feeling joy rushing up within her. 'Are you . . . I mean . . . oh, Adam!'

Again she banged into chairs, bruising her knees and shins as she tried to hurry across the room towards him. He was coming towards her, also pushing chairs out of his way. They met, stared at each other for a second. Then their arms reached out and went around each other. They hugged and squeezed each other, laughing breathlessly. Then they kissed hotly, greedily and, swaying under the onslaught of passion, collapsed on to two nearby chairs, still holding each other.

'When did you come?' Lenore asked.

'This evening. I arrived just before the end of the concert. I stepped inside from the terrace to hear the last movement of the second piece—and thought I was seeing things when at the end of it you stepped from behind the piano to announce the third item.'

'You didn't know I'd be here?' she exclaimed.

'No. I remembered you telling Valerie Baker in this room that you'd be leaving Northport after the first concert, going to Caracas maybe, and I had no reason to believe you'd changed your mind.'

'But didn't Albert ever tell you I was still living in Northport?'

'Why would he? I never asked him about you when I phoned him to ask how things were at the house. And he never talked about you.' Adam's crooked grin mocked himself as well as Albert. 'Neither of us is very communicative, you know.'

'Mmm, I had noticed,' she retorted, giving him a disdainful glare. 'You don't write letters either. You didn't reply to my note. Did you get it?'

He was silent for a moment, looking down at their two hands that were clasped together and resting on his knee. Then suddenly he looked up and straight into her eyes, and she felt for the first time the sense-thrilling impact of his intensely blue stare.

'I couldn't,' he said quietly. 'My feelings about you were too deep for any words I could write. Besides, I thought you'd left Northport, gone away somewhere, and that I'd never find you again.' He raised both hands and held her head between them, still staring down at her. 'It's good to see you, Lenore, at last. It's so good to *see* you,' he whispered.

They kissed again deeply and sweetly, and it was as if the months they had been apart had never been.

'I guess the operation was a success,' Lenore said somewhat breathlessly when they came up for air.

'I can see almost perfectly. I need glasses to read small print, that's all.'

'But you can use a camera again.'

'I sure can,' he said with satisfaction. 'Thank God! That's why I'm here. I'm going away on an assignment and I want to make arrangements about the house.'

She withdrew from him slightly.

'An assignment?' she repeated faintly, fear flooding her mind; fear of the future, *his* future. 'For the same TV network you'd worked for?'

'That's right.' Adam sounded enthusiastic. She had the impression he could hardly wait to be on his way.

'Where?' she whispered. 'Where will you be going?'

'El Salvador again. Nicaragua. The wars there still go on.'

'But . . . but that's where you. . . .' she began, and broke off with a shudder.

'Where Frank got blown to pieces and I was injured,' he finished for her grimly. 'I know. But I have to go back.'

'Why? Why do you hace to go?' she exclaimed, turning to him urgently. 'Isn't there something else you could do? Something less violent?'

'I have to go back,' he said again, quietly. 'I have to go back to prove to myself that I haven't lost my nerve; that I'm not afraid to go among the flying bullets, the mortar bombs, and take pictures of the reality and the pathos of civil war, because that's what it is that's going on down there.'

'But . . . but what about us?' she asked, her head bent and her eyes filling with tears, her hands twisting together on her lap.

'Us?' he repeated queryingly.

'Yes, you and me.' She looked up at him, shaking her hair back from her face. 'Doesn't our . . . our relationship . . . our friendship, whatever you like to call it, matter to you? Does dashing about a war-torn country, filming death and destruction, mean more to you than . . . than I do?'

Adam studied her upturned face and slowly the hardness left his eyes and gave way to a warm sensual glow. He touched her cheek with the tips of his fingers.

'No. Nothing means more to me than you do,' he admitted slowly.

'Then don't go on that assignment,' she cried, throwing her arms about him, holding him closely her cheek pressed against his rough one. 'Don't go, Adam. Stay here with me and make films about music. Oh, please don't go away. You could be hurt again—you could be killed!'

He didn't say anything but held her for a while, quietly stroking her hair until, comforted, she calmed down, resting her head against his shoulder, feeling the warmth of him spreading through her. Then he said firmly,

'I have to go, Lenore. I'll never be at peace with myself unless I go back and finish what Frank and I were trying to do.' He paused, then added softly, 'If you love me you'll try to understand how I feel about going back and why I have to do it.'

Lenore was silent then, thinking about what he had said and acknowledging reluctantly that he was right.

'When? When will you go?' she asked at last in a lifeless voice.

'The beginning of October.'

A month. They had a whole month to be together.

'Did you get a letter from Isaac and Jack?' she asked, lifting her head from his shoulder and pushing away from him. Leaning against him, feeling the life-force pulsing through him, was having its usual weakening effect on her. If she stayed in his arms much longer she would succumb to desire and begin to make love to him, and she wasn't going to do that. Not yet, anyway.

'Yes, I did,' he replied. 'I'm hoping to meet with them some time next week.'

'You could have seen them tonight and discussed the matter,' she pointed out.

'I could, but once I'd seen you I didn't want to talk with them until I'd talked with you first. I'd have come to the Inn tomorrow if you hadn't come back into the house.' Adam slanted her a curious glance. 'Why did you come back?'

'I thought Albert had gone and had left the front door open, so I came in to shut it.' She decided to say nothing of having felt his presence in the house, so she had returned to it, hoping to find him. 'How did you know I'd come in?'

'I saw you. I was in the study and was just coming to shut the front door. When you stepped into this room I shut the door and locked it. You came into the hallway and I stayed hidden in the shadows?'

'Why? Why didn't you speak to me then?'

'To tease you a little, I guess.'

'You scared the life out of me when you did speak,' she retorted. 'I thought I was imagining things.' She glanced at the open windows. 'I must go, Blythe will be wondering where I am.'

'Call her and tell her you won't be back tonight,' said Adam autocratically, getting to his feet. Taking hold of one of her hands, he pulled her to her feet. 'The phone is in the study. Come on.'

'But . . . I. . . .'

'No buts,' he interrupted her curtly. 'You're staying the night here. With me.' Making for the door, he pulled her after him and in the darkness of the hall he stopped, swinging her round and against him. Her breasts tingled as they were crushed against his hard chest. His hands pressed urgently against the sides of her breasts, before sweeping down to her waist, her hips. Fingers digging into her buttocks, he dragged the lower part of her body against his hips so that she felt his arousal. Her legs shook and she seemed to melt against him.

'We've got a lot of catching up to do,' he whispered into the softness of her hair. 'I've been wanting you a hell of a long time, ever since I left you here in my bed that morning. It took all my will power to leave you, but I had to do it. I had to have that operation.' He paused, breathing heavily and shakily as he tried to control the desire that was throbbing through him. 'There's been no one else these past three months,' he continued. 'No one else but you, in my mind, in my body, haunting me, tormenting me.'

'It's been like that for me too,' whispered Lenore, helpless now and clinging to him.

'Then what are we standing here for? Let's go to bed,' he growled roughly, and taking her hand again began to pull her towards the stairs.

'But what about Blythe?' she protested, holding back, trying to pull her hand free of his.

'Later. You can call her later,' he said, tugging on her hand so hard she went towards him in a little involuntary rush, colliding with him. Dropping her hand, he swept her up into his arms and started up the stairs, and she didn't protest any more.

In the bedroom, on the wide bed, they entered their own secret world; a world of soft sensuous caresses and tender titillating kisses. Slowly and reverently it began, like the beginning of a piece of music, and gradually the rhythm increased as the beat of their hearts grew faster and the blood boiled in their veins. Faster and faster, louder and louder, until suddenly they were united in a single thunderous chord that seemed to split the darkness. And then slowly, beautifully, it ended—a quiet unwinding of tension to the accompaniment of whispered endearments and the low-voiced mutual confession of love.

This time neither left the other. They loved together, they slept together and they woke together, turning to each other to kiss and fondle lazily in the mellow golden light of the September morning.

'Why didn't you leave Northport after that first concert?' asked Adam. 'Why didn't you go to Caracas?'

'I wasn't appointed to the orchestra there,' she explained. 'I'm going to stay here. I've been producing the concerts for the public TV network since Valerie left.' She gave him a cautious sidelong glance. 'You knew she'd left, and went back to New York?' she asked.

'I know,' he replied coolly. 'Go on about this producing you've been doing. Are you any good at it?'

'Jim Lorway thinks so, and the manager of the network thinks so too. They've asked me to produce more programmes for them. And then ... next summer ... if somewhere can be found where it can be held the music group wants me to organise the music and arts festival.' She laid a hand tentatively on his bare arm and let her fingers slide over the warm hairy skin. 'Adam, have you decided? Are you going to allow the festival to take place here in this house?'

'I might,' he drawled. His eyes were closed, the

heavy lids fringed by thick bronze-coloured lashes. 'A lot depends on you.'

'We seem to have had this conversation before,' she murmured, her heart beginning to thump excitedly. Slowly Adam's eyelids lifted. Half closed, his eyes laughed at her.

'We have,' he replied. 'Marry me, Lenore, and live here, and you can have all the music groups in the world to play here whenever you like. I think that's what I said to you, and you accused me of not being normal.' His mouth twisted bitterly.

'Oh, will you ever forgive me for saying that?' she wailed, burying her face against the hardness of his shoulder. 'I didn't mean that I wouldn't marry you because you were half blind. I meant that I couldn't accept your proposal because I felt you wouldn't have asked me to marry you if you hadn't been half blind—would you?' She raised her head to look at him challengingly.

'If I hadn't been half blind I wouldn't have been here and I wouldn't have met you, so you're partly right,' he said dryly. 'And I wouldn't have proposed to you. But now I'm not half blind and I'm as normal as I'll ever be, and I'm proposing again. Lenore, will you marry me before I go away?'

'Why?' she whispered. 'Why?'

'For the same reason I asked you before,' he replied impatiently. 'Good God, woman, do I have to spell it out in words of one syllable? I want to legalise whatever it is that's going on between us. What sort of a guy do you think I am? Do you think I'm the sort who sleeps around promiscuously without caring, without loving? I

want to marry for all the usual reasons a man
wants to marry a woman. I like being with you
and I want to make sure that you're mine and
only mine. I want to have the right to come home
to you and live with you whenever I can. I want
to look after you, protect you. I want to share this
house with you. I want to give it to you and let
you turn it into a music centre. I want to marry
you because ... because ... Oh, hell, I guess it's
because I love you. So what's your answer?' This
time his eyes glittered with passion. 'You haven't
found some other guy you prefer to me, have
you?' he demanded suspiciously.

'No, no—oh no, I haven't,' Lenore replied
quickly. 'Would I be here with you now if I had?
Would I have done with you what we did in the
night if I had? Oh, Adam, I can only love one man
at a time, and you're the only man I've ever loved
like this, with ... with a sort of desperate desire.'

'Then you'll marry me and give me the right to
come home to you when my assignment is
through?'

'Yes, I'll marry you,' she whispered. 'But
you'll have to promise to be careful and not to get
killed or hurt.'

'I promise,' Adam murmured, gathering her
against him. 'Knowing you're here for me to
come home to is going to make all the difference
to my way of living; all the difference in the
world,' he whispered.

They were married three days before he left for
El Salvador. Blythe and Josh were present at the
ceremony and so were Albert and Bertha. Most
of the music group were there too, and Ella

Parini, Lenore's and Blythe's mother, newly arrived from Scotland and a little critical of Lenore's decision to marry Adam.

'He seems most unsuitable to be a husband,' she complained to Lenore at the reception that was held at the Inn.

'I love him,' said Lenore simply, as if that explained everything.

'But he's going away so soon, going to leave you for three whole months. That's hardly the way to start a marriage,' said Mrs Parini. 'He should stay with you, change his job so that he can live with you all the time. You know, Lenore, you're very like your father—impulsive. It must be the Italian blood showing.' Her glance slid away from Adam who was talking to Isaac and drifted on to Blythe who was standing nearby with Josh. 'Now, Blythe is much more like me,' she went on, her eyes softening with affection as they lingered on her elder daughter. 'And I much prefer her choice of husband. I expect she'll give up this place when she's married and will settle down to have children.'

'Oh, I doubt it,' retorted Lenore. 'I mean, I doubt she'll give up the Inn when she marries Josh. She enjoys managing it too much, and she'll fit the babies in somehow when they come.' She glanced across at Adam again. 'And so will I, one day,' she added softly.

And feeling the intense sense-arousing shock of Adam's intense blue stare, she left her mother's side and walked across to him, lifting her face to his as if inviting him to kiss her.

'We don't have much time left,' he murmured. 'Shall we leave them all now and go home?'

A few minutes later they were driving to the old house on the point. Against grey sky and grey sea it loomed a darker grey, in one of its mysterious moods. They went in and closed the door, to enter their own secret world, a world of light and harmony that they had created themselves from their desperate desire for each other; a world in which and of which they were and to which they would always return whenever they were together.

Harlequin Photo ⇜ Calendar ⇝

Turn Your Favorite Photo into a Calendar.

JULY 1984

The Browns

Uniquely yours, this 10x17½" calendar features your favorite photograph, with any name you wish in attractive lettering at the bottom. A delightfully personal and practical idea!

Send us your favorite color print, black-and-white print, negative, or slide, any size (we'll return it), along with 3 proofs of purchase (coupon below) from a June or July release of Harlequin Romance, Harlequin Presents, Harlequin Superromance, Harlequin American Romance or Harlequin Temptation, plus $5.75 (includes shipping and handling).

Harlequin Photo Calendar Offer
(PROOF OF PURCHASE)

NAME_____

(Please Print)

ADDRESS_____

CITY_____ STATE_____ ZIP_____

NAME ON CALENDAR_____

Mail photo, 3 proofs, plus check or money order for $5.75 payable to:	**Harlequin Books** P.O. Box 52020 Phoenix, AZ 85072	2-5

Offer expires December 31, 1984. (Not available in Canada)   CAL-1